# Victorian Short Stories

## Stories of Successful Marriages

**Elizabeth Gaskell et al**

**Victorian Short Stories: Stories of Successful Marriages**

ISBN: 978-1-63637-465-9

# CONTENTS

# CONTENTS

# ELIZABETH GASKELL

## THE MANCHESTER MARRIAGE

### (Household Words, Christmas 1858)

Mr and Mrs Openshaw came from Manchester to settle in London. He had been, what is called in Lancashire, a salesman for a large manufacturing firm, who were extending their business, and opening a warehouse in the city; where Mr Openshaw was now to superintend their affairs. He rather enjoyed the change; having a kind of curiosity about London, which he had never yet been able to gratify in his brief visits to the metropolis. At the same time, he had an odd, shrewd contempt for the inhabitants, whom he always pictured to himself as fine, lazy people, caring nothing but for fashion and aristocracy, and lounging away their days in Bond Street, and such places; ruining good English, and ready in their turn to despise him as a provincial. The hours that the men of business kept in the city scandalized him too, accustomed as he was to the early dinners of Manchester folk and the consequently far longer evenings. Still, he was pleased to go to London, though he would not for the world have confessed it, even to himself, and always spoke of the step to his friends as one demanded of him by the interests of his employers, and sweetened to him by a considerable increase of salary. This, indeed, was so liberal that he

1

might have been justified in taking a much larger house than the one he did, had he not thought himself bound to set an example to Londoners of how little a Manchester man of business cared for show. Inside, however, he furnished it with an unusual degree of comfort, and, in the winter-time, he insisted on keeping up as large fires as the grates would allow, in every room where the temperature was in the least chilly. Moreover, his northern sense of hospitality was such that, if he were at home, he could hardly suffer a visitor to leave the house without forcing meat and drink upon him. Every servant in the house was well warmed, well fed, and kindly treated; for their master scorned all petty saving in aught that conduced to comfort; while he amused himself by following out all his accustomed habits and individual ways, in defiance of what any of his new neighbours might think.

His wife was a pretty, gentle woman, of suitable age and character. He was forty-two, she thirty-five. He was loud and decided; she soft and yielding. They had two children; or rather, I should say, she had two; for the elder, a girl of eleven, was Mrs Openshaw's child by Frank Wilson, her first husband. The younger was a little boy, Edwin, who could just prattle, and to whom his father delighted to speak in the broadest and most unintelligible Lancashire dialect, in order to keep up what he called the true Saxon accent.

Mrs Openshaw's Christian name was Alice, and her first husband had been her own cousin. She was the orphan niece of a sea-captain in Liverpool; a quiet, grave little creature, of great personal attraction when she was fifteen or sixteen, with regular features and a blooming complexion. But she was very shy, and believed herself to be very stupid and awkward; and was frequently scolded by her

2

aunt, her own uncle's second wife. So when her cousin, Frank Wilson, came home from a long absence at sea, and first was kind and protective to her; secondly, attentive; and thirdly, desperately in love with her, she hardly knew how to be grateful enough to him. It is true, she would have preferred his remaining in the first or second stages of behaviour; for his violent love puzzled and frightened her. Her uncle neither helped nor hindered the love affair, though it was going on under his own eyes. Frank's stepmother had such a variable temper, that there was no knowing whether what she liked one day she would like the next, or not. At length she went to such extremes of crossness that Alice was only too glad to shut her eyes and rush blindly at the chance of escape from domestic tyranny offered her by a marriage with her cousin; and, liking him better than any one in the world, except her uncle (who was at this time at sea), she went off one morning and was married to him, her only bridesmaid being the housemaid at her aunt's. The consequence was that Frank and his wife went into lodgings, and Mrs Wilson refused to see them, and turned away Norah, the warm-hearted housemaid, whom they accordingly took into their service. When Captain Wilson returned from his voyage he was very cordial with the young couple, and spent many an evening at their lodgings, smoking his pipe and sipping his grog; but he told them, for quietness' sake, he could not ask them to his own house; for his wife was bitter against them. They were not, however, very unhappy about this.

The seed of future unhappiness lay rather in Frank's vehement, passionate disposition, which led him to resent his wife's shyness and want of demonstrativeness as failures in conjugal duty. He was already tormenting himself, and her too in a slighter degree, by apprehensions and imaginations of what might befall her during

3

his approaching absence at sea. At last, he went to his father and urged him to insist upon Alice's being once more received under his roof; the more especially as there was now a prospect of her confinement while her husband was away on his voyage. Captain Wilson was, as he himself expressed it, 'breaking up', and unwilling to undergo the excitement of a scene; yet he felt that what his son said was true. So he went to his wife. And before Frank set sail, he had the comfort of seeing his wife installed in her old little garret in his father's house. To have placed her in the one best spare room was a step beyond Mrs Wilson's powers of submission or generosity. The worst part about it, however, was that the faithful Norah had to be dismissed. Her place as housemaid had been filled up; and, even if it had not, she had forfeited Mrs Wilson's good opinion for ever. She comforted her young master and mistress by pleasant prophecies of the time when they would have a household of their own; of which, whatever service she might be in meanwhile, she should be sure to form a part. Almost the last action Frank did, before setting sail, was going with Alice to see Norah once more at her mother's house; and then he went away.

Alice's father-in-law grew more and more feeble as winter advanced. She was of great use to her stepmother in nursing and amusing him; and although there was anxiety enough in the household, there was, perhaps, more of peace than there had been for years, for Mrs Wilson had not a bad heart, and was softened by the visible approach of death to one whom she loved, and touched by the lonely condition of the young creature expecting her first confinement in her husband's absence. To this relenting mood Norah owed the permission to come and nurse Alice when her baby was born, and to remain and attend on Captain Wilson.

Before one letter had been received from Frank (who had sailed for the East Indies and China), his father died. Alice was always glad to remember that he had held her baby in his arms, and kissed and blessed it before his death. After that, and the consequent examination into the state of his affairs, it was found that he had left far less property than people had been led by his style of living to expect; and what money there was, was settled all upon his wife, and at her disposal after her death. This did not signify much to Alice, as Frank was now first mate of his ship, and, in another voyage or two, would be captain. Meanwhile he had left her rather more than two hundred pounds (all his savings) in the bank.

It became time for Alice to hear from her husband. One letter from the Cape she had already received. The next was to announce his arrival in India. As week after week passed over, and no intelligence of the ship having got there reached the office of the owners, and the captain's wife was in the same state of ignorant suspense as Alice herself, her fears grew most oppressive. At length the day came when, in reply to her inquiry at the shipping office, they told her that the owners had given up hope of ever hearing more of the Betsy-Jane and had sent in their claim upon the underwriters. Now that he was gone for ever, she first felt a yearning, longing love for the kind cousin, the dear friend, the sympathizing protector, whom she should never see again;—first felt a passionate desire to show him his child, whom she had hitherto rather craved to have all to herself—her own sole possession. Her grief was, however, noiseless and quiet—rather to the scandal of Mrs Wilson who bewailed her stepson as if he and she had always lived together in perfect harmony, and who evidently thought it her duty to burst into fresh tears at every strange face she saw; dwelling on his poor young widow's desolate state, and the helplessness of the fatherless child, with an unction as if she liked the excitement of the sorrowful story.

So passed away the first days of Alice's widowhood. By and by things subsided into their natural and tranquil course. But, as if the young creature was always to be in some heavy trouble, her ewe-lamb began to be ailing, pining, and sickly. The child's mysterious illness turned out to be some affection of the spine, likely to affect health but not to shorten life—at least, so the doctors said. But the long, dreary suffering of one whom a mother loves as Alice loved her only child, is hard to look forward to. Only Norah guessed what Alice suffered; no one but God knew.

And so it fell out, that when Mrs Wilson, the elder, came to her one day, in violent distress, occasioned by a very material diminution in the value of the property that her husband had left her—a diminution which made her income barely enough to support herself, much less Alice—the latter could hardly understand how anything which did not touch health or life could cause such grief; and she received the intelligence with irritating composure. But when, that afternoon, the little sick child was brought in, and the grandmother—who, after all, loved it well—began a fresh moan over her losses to its unconscious ears—saying how she had planned to consult this or that doctor, and to give it this or that comfort or luxury in after years, but that now all chance of this had passed away—Alice's heart was touched, and she drew near to Mrs Wilson with unwonted caresses, and, in a spirit not unlike to that of Ruth, entreated that, come what would, they might remain together. After much discussion in succeeding days, it was arranged that Mrs Wilson should take a house in Manchester, furnishing it partly with what furniture she had, and providing the rest with Alice's remaining two hundred pounds. Mrs Wilson was herself a Manchester woman, and naturally longed to return to her native town; some connexions of her own, too, at that time required lodgings, for which they were willing to pay pretty handsomely. Alice undertook the active superintendence and superior work of the household; Norah—willing, faithful Norah—offered to cook, scour, do anything in short, so that she might but remain with them.

The plan succeeded. For some years their first lodgers remained with them, and all went smoothly—with that one sad exception of the little girl's increasing deformity. How that mother loved that child, it is not for words to tell!

Then came a break of misfortune. Their lodgers left, and no one succeeded to them. After some months, it became necessary to remove to a smaller house; and Alice's tender conscience was torn by the idea that she ought not to be a burden to her mother-in-law, but to go out and seek her own maintenance. And leave her child! The thought came like the sweeping boom of a funeral-bell over her heart.

By and by, Mr Openshaw came to lodge with them. He had started in life as the errand-boy and sweeper-out of a warehouse; had struggled up through all the grades of employment in it, fighting his way through the hard, striving Manchester life with strong, pushing energy of character. Every spare moment of time had been sternly given up to self-teaching. He was a capital accountant, a good French and German scholar, a keen, far-seeing tradesman— understanding markets and the bearing of events, both near and distant, on trade; and yet, with such vivid attention to present details, that I do not think he ever saw a group of flowers in the fields without thinking whether their colour would, or would not, form harmonious contrasts in the coming spring muslins and prints. He went to debating societies, and threw himself with all his heart and soul into politics; esteeming, it must be owned, every man a fool or a knave who differed from him, and overthrowing his opponents rather by the loud strength of his language than the calm strength of his logic. There was something of the Yankee in all this. Indeed, his theory ran parallel to the famous Yankee motto— 'England flogs creation, and Manchester flogs England.' Such a man, as may be fancied, had had no time for falling in love, or any such nonsense. At the age when most young men go through their courting and matrimony, he had not the means of keeping a wife, and was far too practical to think of having one. And now that he was in easy circumstances, a rising man, he considered women almost as encumbrances to the world, with whom a man had better have as little to do as possible. His first impression of Alice was indistinct, and he did not care enough about her to make it distinct. 'A pretty, yea-nay kind of woman', would have been his description of her, if he had been pushed into a corner. He was rather afraid, in the beginning, that her quiet ways arose from a listlessness and laziness of character, which would have been exceedingly discordant to his active, energetic nature. But, when he found out the punctuality with which his wishes were attended to, and her work was done; when he was called in the morning at the very stroke of the clock, his shaving-water scalding hot, his fire bright, his coffee made exactly as his peculiar fancy dictated (for he was a man who had his theory about everything based upon what he knew of science, and often perfectly original)—then he began to think: not that Alice had any particular merit, but that he had got into remarkably good lodgings; his restlessness wore away, and he began to consider himself as almost settled for life in them.

Mr Openshaw had been too busy, all his days, to be introspective. He did not know that he had any tenderness in his nature; and if he had become conscious of its abstract existence he would have considered it as a manifestation of disease in some part of him. But he was decoyed into pity unawares; and pity led on to tenderness. That little helpless child—always carried about by one of the three busy women of the house, or else patiently threading coloured beads in the chair from which, by no effort of its own, could it ever move—the great grave blue eyes, full of serious, not uncheerful, expression, giving to the small delicate face a look beyond its years—the soft plaintive voice dropping out but few words, so unlike the continual prattle of a child—caught Mr Openshaw's attention in spite of himself. One day—he half scorned himself for doing so—he cut short his dinner-hour to go in search of some toy, which should take the place of those eternal beads. I forget what he bought; but, when he gave the present (which he took care to do in a short abrupt manner, and when no one was by to see him), he was almost thrilled by the flash of delight that came over that child's face, and he could not help, all through that afternoon, going over and over again the picture left on his memory, by the bright effect of unexpected joy on the little girl's face. When he returned home, he found his slippers placed by his sitting-room fire; and even more careful attention paid to his fancies than was habitual in those model lodgings. When Alice had taken the last of his tea-things away—she had been silent as usual till then—she stood for an instant with the door in her hand. Mr Openshaw looked as if he were deep in his book, though in fact he did not see a line; but was heartily wishing the woman would go, and not make any palaver of gratitude. But she only said:

'I am very much obliged to you, sir. Thank you very much,' and was gone, even before he could send her away with a 'There, my good woman, that's enough!'

9

For some time longer he took no apparent notice of the child. He even hardened his heart into disregarding her sudden flush of colour and little timid smile of recognition, when he saw her by chance. But, after all, this could not last for ever; and, having a second time given way to tenderness, there was no relapse. The insidious enemy having thus entered his heart, in the guise of compassion to the child, soon assumed the more dangerous form of interest in the mother. He was aware of this change of feeling — despised himself for it — struggled with it; nay, internally yielded to it and cherished it, long before he suffered the slightest expression of it, by word, action, or look to escape him. He watched Alice's docile, obedient ways to her stepmother; the love which she had inspired in the rough Norah (roughened by the wear and tear of sorrow and years); but, above all, he saw the wild, deep, passionate affection existing between her and her child. They spoke little to anyone else, or when anyone else was by; but, when alone together, they talked, and murmured, and cooed, and chattered so continually, that Mr Openshaw first wondered what they could find to say to each other, and next became irritated because they were always so grave and silent with him. All this time he was perpetually devising small new pleasures for the child. His thoughts ran, in a pertinacious way, upon the desolate life before her; and often he came back from his day's work loaded with the very thing Alice had been longing for, but had not been able to procure. One time, it was a little chair for drawing the little sufferer along the streets; and, many an evening that following summer, Mr Openshaw drew her along himself, regardless of the remarks of his acquaintances. One day in autumn, he put down his newspaper, as Alice came in with the breakfast, and said, in as indifferent a voice as he could assume:

10

'Mrs Frank, is there any reason why we two should not put up our horses together?'

Alice stood still in perplexed wonder. What did he mean? He had resumed the reading of his newspaper, as if he did not expect any answer; so she found silence her safest course, and went on quietly arranging his breakfast, without another word passing between them. Just as he was leaving the house, to go to the warehouse as usual, he turned back and put his head into the bright, neat, tidy kitchen, where all the women breakfasted in the morning:

'You'll think of what I said, Mrs Frank' (this was her name with the lodgers), 'and let me have your opinion upon it tonight.'

Alice was thankful that her mother and Norah were too busy talking together to attend much to this speech. She determined not to think about it at all through the day; and, of course, the effort not to think made her think all the more. At night she sent up Norah with his tea. But Mr Openshaw almost knocked Norah down as she was going out at the door, by pushing past her and calling out, 'Mrs Frank!' in an impatient voice, at the top of the stairs.

Alice went up, rather than seem to have affixed too much meaning to his words.

'Well, Mrs Frank,' he said, 'what answer? Don't make it too long; for I have lots of office work to get through tonight.'

'I hardly know what you meant, sir,' said truthful Alice.

'Well! I should have thought you might have guessed. You're not new at this sort of work, and I am. However, I'll make it plain this time. Will you have me to be thy wedded husband, and serve me,

11

and love me, and honour me, and all that sort of thing? Because, if you will, I will do as much by you, and be a father to your child—and that's more than is put in the prayer-book. Now, I'm a man of my word; and what I say, I feel; and what I promise, I'll do. Now, for your answer!'

Alice was silent. He began to make the tea, as if her reply was a matter of perfect indifference to him; but, as soon as that was done, he became impatient.

'Well?' said he.

'How long, sir, may I have to think over it?'

'Three minutes!' (looking at his watch). 'You've had two already—that makes five. Be a sensible woman, say Yes, and sit down to tea with me, and we'll talk it over together; for, after tea, I shall be busy; say No' (he hesitated a moment to try and keep his voice in the same tone), 'and I shan't say another word about it, but pay up a year's rent for my rooms tomorrow, and be off. Time's up! Yes or no?'

'If you please, sir—you have been so good to little Ailsie—'

'There, sit down comfortably by me on the sofa, and let's have our tea together. I am glad to find you are as good and sensible as I took you for.'

And this was Alice Wilson's second wooing.

Mr Openshaw's will was too strong, and his circumstances too good, for him not to carry all before him. He settled Mrs Wilson in a comfortable house of her own, and made her quite independent of lodgers. The little that Alice said with regard to future plans was in Norah's behalf.

12

'No,' said Mr Openshaw. 'Norah shall take care of the old lady as long as she lives; and, after that, she shall either come and live with us, or, if she likes it better, she shall have a provision for life—for your sake, missus. No one who has been good to you or the child shall go unrewarded. But even the little one will be better for some fresh stuff about her. Get her a bright, sensible girl as a nurse; one who won't go rubbing her with calf's-foot jelly as Norah does; wasting good stuff outside that ought to go in, but will follow doctors' directions; which, as you must see pretty clearly by this time, Norah won't; because they give the poor little wench pain. Now, I'm not above being nesh for other folks myself. I can stand a good blow, and never change colour; but, set me in the operating room in the infirmary, and I turn as sick as a girl. Yet, if need were, I would hold the little wench on my knees while she screeched with pain, if it were to do her poor back good. Nay, nay, wench! keep your white looks for the time when it comes—I don't say it ever will. But this I know, Norah will spare the child and cheat the doctor, if she can. Now, I say, give the bairn a year or two's chance, and then, when the pack of doctors have done their best—and, maybe, the old lady has gone—we'll have Norah back or do better for her.'

The pack of doctors could do no good to little Ailsie. She was beyond their power. But her father (for so he insisted on being called, and also on Alice's no longer retaining the appellation of Mamma, but becoming henceforward Mother), by his healthy cheerfulness of manner, his clear decision of purpose, his odd turns and quirks of humour, added to his real strong love for the helpless little girl, infused a new element of brightness and confidence into her life; and, though her back remained the same, her general health was strengthened, and Alice—never going beyond a smile herself—had the pleasure of seeing her child taught to laugh.

As for Alice's own life, it was happier than it had ever been before. Mr Openshaw required no demonstration, no expressions of affection from her. Indeed, these would rather have disgusted him. Alice could love deeply, but could not talk about it. The perpetual requirement of loving words, looks, and caresses, and misconstruing their absence into absence of love, had been the great trial of her former married life. Now, all went on clear and straight, under the guidance of her husband's strong sense, warm heart, and powerful will. Year by year their worldly prosperity increased. At Mrs Wilson's death, Norah came back to them as nurse to the newly-born little Edwin; into which post she was not installed without a pretty strong oration on the part of the proud and happy father, who declared that if he found out that Norah ever tried to screen the boy by a falsehood, or to make him nesh either in body or mind, she should go that very day. Norah and Mr Openshaw were not on the most thoroughly cordial terms; neither of them fully recognizing or appreciating the other's best qualities.

This was the previous history of the Lancashire family who had now removed to London.

They had been there about a year, when Mr Openshaw suddenly informed his wife that he had determined to heal long-standing feuds, and had asked his uncle and aunt Chadwick to come and pay them a visit and see London. Mrs Openshaw had never seen this uncle and aunt of her husband's. Years before she had married him, there had been a quarrel. All she knew was, that Mr Chadwick was a small manufacturer in a country town in South Lancashire. She was extremely pleased that the breach was to be healed, and began making preparations to render their visit pleasant.

They arrived at last. Going to see London was such an event to

14

them, that Mrs Chadwick had made all new linen fresh for the occasion—from night-caps downwards; and as for gowns, ribbons, and collars, she might have been going into the wilds of Canada where never a shop is, so large was her stock. A fortnight before the day of her departure for London, she had formally called to take leave of all her acquaintance; saying she should need every bit of the intermediate time for packing up. It was like a second wedding in her imagination; and, to complete the resemblance which an entirely new wardrobe made between the two events, her husband brought her back from Manchester, on the last market-day before they set off, a gorgeous pearl and amethyst brooch, saying, 'Lunnon should see that Lancashire folks knew a handsome thing when they saw it.'

For some time after Mr and Mrs Chadwick arrived at the Openshaws' there was no opportunity for wearing this brooch; but at length they obtained an order to see Buckingham Palace, and the spirit of loyalty demanded that Mrs Chadwick should wear her best clothes in visiting the abode of her sovereign. On her return she hastily changed her dress; for Mr Openshaw had planned that they should go to Richmond, drink tea, and return by moonlight. Accordingly, about five o'clock, Mr and Mrs Openshaw and Mr and Mrs Chadwick set off.

The housemaid and cook sat below, Norah hardly knew where. She was always engrossed in the nursery in tending her two children, and in sitting by the restless, excitable Ailsie till she fell asleep. By and by the housemaid Bessy tapped gently at the door. Norah went to her, and they spoke in whispers.

'Nurse! there's someone downstairs wants you.'

'Wants me! who is it?'

'A gentleman—'

'A gentleman? Nonsense!'

'Well! a man, then, and he asks for you, and he rang at the front-door bell, and has walked into the dining-room.'

'You should never have let him,' exclaimed Norah. 'Master and missus out—'

'I did not want him to come in; but, when he heard you lived here, he walked past me, and sat down on the first chair, and said, "Tell her to come and speak to me." There is no gas lighted in the room, and supper is all set out.'

'He'll be off with the spoons!' exclaimed Norah, putting the housemaid's fear into words, and preparing to leave the room; first, however, giving a look to Ailsie, sleeping soundly and calmly.

Downstairs she went, uneasy fears stirring in her bosom. Before she entered the dining-room she provided herself with a candle, and, with it in her hand, she went in, looking around her in the darkness for her visitor.

He was standing up, holding by the table. Norah and he looked at each other; gradual recognition coming into their eyes.

'Norah?' at length he asked.

'Who are you?' asked Norah, with the sharp tones of alarm and incredulity. 'I don't know you'; trying, by futile words of disbelief, to do away with the terrible fact before her.

'Am I so changed?' he said pathetically. 'I dare say I am. But, Norah, tell me!' he breathed hard, 'where is my wife? Is she—is she alive?'

16

He came nearer to Norah, and would have taken her hand; but she backed away from him; looking at him all the time with staring eyes, as if he were some horrible object. Yet he was a handsome, bronzed, good-looking fellow, with beard and moustache, giving him a foreign-looking aspect; but his eyes! there was no mistaking those eager, beautiful eyes—the very same that Norah had watched not half an hour ago, till sleep stole softly over them.

'Tell me, Norah—I can bear it—I have feared it so often. Is she dead?' Norah still kept silence. 'She is dead!' He hung on Norah's words and looks, as if for confirmation or contradiction.

'What shall I do?' groaned Norah. 'Oh, sir! why did you come? how did you find me out? where have you been? We thought you dead, we did indeed!' She poured out words and questions to gain time, as if time would help her.

'Norah! answer me this question straight, by yes or no—Is my wife dead?'

'No, she is not,' said Norah, slowly and heavily.

'Oh, what a relief! Did she receive my letters? But perhaps you don't know. Why did you leave her? Where is she? Oh, Norah, tell me all quickly!'

'Mr Frank!' said Norah at last, almost driven to bay by her terror lest her mistress should return at any moment and find him there— unable to consider what was best to be done or said—rushing at something decisive, because she could not endure her present state: 'Mr Frank! we never heard a line from you, and the shipowners said you had gone down, you and everyone else. We thought you were dead, if ever man was, and poor Miss Alice and her little sick,

17

helpless child! Oh, sir, you must guess it,' cried the poor creature at last, bursting out into a passionate fit of crying, 'for indeed I cannot tell it. But it was no one's fault. God help us all this night!'

Norah had sat down. She trembled too much to stand. He took her hands in his. He squeezed them hard, as if, by physical pressure, the truth could be wrung out.

'Norah.' This time his tone was calm, stagnant as despair. 'She has married again!'

Norah shook her head sadly. The grasp slowly relaxed. The man had fainted.

There was brandy in the room. Norah forced some drops into Mr Frank's mouth, chafed his hands, and—when mere animal life returned, before the mind poured in its flood of memories and thoughts—she lifted him up, and rested his head against her knees. Then she put a few crumbs of bread taken from the supper-table, soaked in brandy, into his mouth. Suddenly he sprang to his feet.

'Where is she? Tell me this instant.' He looked so wild, so mad, so desperate, that Norah felt herself to be in bodily danger; but her time of dread had gone by. She had been afraid to tell him the truth, and then she had been a coward. Now, her wits were sharpened by the sense of his desperate state. He must leave the house. She would pity him afterwards; but now she must rather command and upbraid; for he must leave the house before her mistress came home. That one necessity stood clear before her.

'She is not here: that is enough for you to know. Nor can I say exactly where she is' (which was true to the letter if not to the spirit). 'Go away, and tell me where to find you tomorrow, and I

18

will tell you all. My master and mistress may come back at any minute, and then what would become of me, with a strange man in the house?'

Such an argument was too petty to touch his excited mind.

'I don't care for your master and mistress. If your master is a man, he must feel for me—poor shipwrecked sailor that I am—kept for years a prisoner amongst savages, always, always, always thinking of my wife and my home—dreaming of her by night, talking to her though she could not hear, by day. I loved her more than all heaven and earth put together. Tell me where she is, this instant, you wretched woman, who salved over her wickedness to her, as you do to me!'

The clock struck ten. Desperate positions require desperate measures.

'If you will leave the house now, I will come to you tomorrow and tell you all. What is more, you shall see your child now. She lies sleeping upstairs. Oh, sir, you have a child, you do not know that as yet—a little weakly girl—with just a heart and soul beyond her years. We have reared her up with such care! We watched her, for we thought for many a year she might die any day, and we tended her, and no hard thing has come near her, and no rough word has ever been said to her. And now you come and will take her life into your hand, and will crush it. Strangers to her have been kind to her; but her own father—Mr Frank, I am her nurse, and I love her, and I tend her, and I would do anything for her that I could. Her mother's heart beats as hers beats; and, if she suffers a pain, her mother trembles all over. If she is happy, it is her mother that smiles and is glad. If she is growing stronger, her mother is healthy: if she

19

dwindles, her mother languishes. If she dies—well, I don't know; it is not everyone can lie down and die when they wish it. Come upstairs, Mr Frank, and see your child. Seeing her will do good to your poor heart. Then go away, in God's name, just this one night; tomorrow, if need be, you can do anything—kill us all if you will, or show yourself a great, grand man, whom God will bless for ever and ever. Come, Mr Frank, the look of a sleeping child is sure to give peace.'

She led him upstairs; at first almost helping his steps, till they came near the nursery door. She had wellnigh forgotten the existence of little Edwin. It struck upon her with affright as the shaded light fell over the other cot; but she skilfully threw that corner of the room into darkness, and let the light fall on the sleeping Ailsie. The child had thrown down the coverings, and her deformity, as she lay with her back to them, was plainly visible through her slight nightgown. Her little face, deprived of the lustre of her eyes, looked wan and pinched, and had a pathetic expression in it, even as she slept. The poor father looked and looked with hungry, wistful eyes, into which the big tears came swelling up slowly and dropped heavily down, as he stood trembling and shaking all over. Norah was angry with herself for growing impatient of the length of time that long lingering gaze lasted. She thought that she waited for full half an hour before Frank stirred. And then—instead of going away—he sank down on his knees by the bedside, and buried his face in the clothes. Little Ailsie stirred uneasily. Norah pulled him up in terror. She could afford no more time, even for prayer, in her extremity of fear; for surely the next moment would bring her mistress home. She took him forcibly by the arm; but, as he was going, his eye lighted on the other bed; he stopped. Intelligence came back into his face. His hands clenched.

'His child?' he asked.

'Her child,' replied Norah. 'God watches over him,' she said instinctively; for Frank's looks excited her fears, and she needed to remind herself of the Protector of the helpless.

'God has not watched over me,' he said, in despair; his thoughts apparently recoiling on his own desolate, deserted state. But Norah had no time for pity. Tomorrow she would be as compassionate as her heart prompted. At length she guided him downstairs, and shut the outer door, and bolted it—as if by bolts to keep out facts.

Then she went back into the dining-room, and effaced all traces of his presence, as far as she could. She went upstairs to the nursery and sat there, her head on her hand, thinking what was to come of all this misery. It seemed to her very long before her master and mistress returned; yet it was hardly eleven o'clock. She heard the loud, hearty Lancashire voices on the stairs; and, for the first time, she understood the contrast of the desolation of the poor man who had so lately gone forth in lonely despair.

It almost put her out of patience to see Mrs Openshaw come in, calmly smiling, handsomely dressed, happy, easy, to inquire after her children.

'Did Ailsie go to sleep comfortably?' she whispered to Norah.

'Yes.'

Her mother bent over her, looking at her slumbers with the soft eyes of love. How little she dreamed who had looked on her last! Then she went to Edwin, with perhaps less wistful anxiety in her countenance, but more of pride. She took off her things, to go down to supper. Norah saw her no more that night.

Beside having a door into the passage, the sleeping-nursery opened out of Mr and Mrs Openshaw's room, in order that they might have the children more immediately under their own eyes. Early the next summer's morning, Mrs Openshaw was awakened by Ailsie's startled call of 'Mother! mother!' She sprang up, put on her dressing-gown, and went to her child. Ailsie was only half awake, and in a not unusual state of terror.

'Who was he, mother? Tell me!'

'Who, my darling? No one is here. You have been dreaming, love. Waken up quite. See, it is broad daylight.'

'Yes,' said Ailsie, looking round her; then clinging to her mother, 'but a man was here in the night, mother.'

'Nonsense, little goose. No man has ever come near you!'

'Yes, he did. He stood there. Just by Norah. A man with hair and a beard. And he knelt down and said his prayers. Norah knows he was here, mother' (half angrily, as Mrs Openshaw shook her head in smiling incredulity).

'Well! we will ask Norah when she comes,' said Mrs Openshaw, soothingly. 'But we won't talk any more about him now. It is not five o'clock; it is too early for you to get up. Shall I fetch you a book and read to you?'

'Don't leave me, mother,' said the child, clinging to her. So Mrs Openshaw sat on the bedside talking to Ailsie, and telling her of what they had done at Richmond the evening before, until the little girl's eyes slowly closed and she once more fell asleep.

'What was the matter?' asked Mr Openshaw, as his wife returned to bed.

22

'Ailsie wakened up in a fright, with some story of a man having been in the room to say his prayers—a dream, I suppose.' And no more was said at the time.

Mrs Openshaw had almost forgotten the whole affair when she got up about seven o'clock. But, by and by, she heard a sharp altercation going on in the nursery—Norah speaking angrily to Ailsie, a most unusual thing. Both Mr and Mrs Openshaw listened in astonishment.

'Hold your tongue, Ailsie! let me hear none of your dreams; never let me hear you tell that story again!'

Ailsie began to cry.

Mr Openshaw opened the door of communication, before his wife could say a word.

'Norah, come here!'

The nurse stood at the door, defiant. She perceived she had been heard, but she was desperate.

'Don't let me hear you speak in that manner to Ailsie again,' he said sternly, and shut the door.

Norah was infinitely relieved; for she had dreaded some questioning; and a little blame for sharp speaking was what she could well bear, if cross-examination was let alone.

Downstairs they went, Mr Openshaw carrying Ailsie; the sturdy Edwin coming step by step, right foot foremost, always holding his mother's hand. Each child was placed in a chair by the breakfast-table, and then Mr and Mrs Openshaw stood together at the window, awaiting their visitors' appearance and making plans for the day. There was a pause. Suddenly Mr Openshaw turned to Ailsie, and said:

'What a little goosy somebody is with her dreams, wakening up poor, tired mother in the middle of the night, with a story of a man being in the room.'

'Father! I'm sure I saw him,' said Ailsie, half-crying. 'I don't want to make Norah angry; but I was not asleep, for all she says I was. I had been asleep—and I wakened up quite wide awake, though I was so frightened. I kept my eyes nearly shut, and I saw the man quite plain. A great brown man with a beard. He said his prayers. And then looked at Edwin. And then Norah took him by the arm and led him away, after they had whispered a bit together.'

'Now, my little woman must be reasonable,' said Mr Openshaw, who was always patient with Ailsie. 'There was no man in the house last night at all. No man comes into the house, as you know, if you think; much less goes up into the nursery. But sometimes we dream something has happened, and the dream is so like reality, that you are not the first person, little woman, who has stood out that the thing has really happened.'

'But, indeed, it was not a dream!' said Ailsie, beginning to cry.

Just then Mr and Mrs Chadwick came down, looking grave and discomposed. All during breakfast-time they were silent and uncomfortable. As soon as the breakfast things were taken away, and the children had been carried upstairs, Mr Chadwick began, in an evidently preconcerted manner, to inquire if his nephew was certain that all his servants were honest; for, that Mrs Chadwick had that morning missed a very valuable brooch, which she had worn the day before. She remembered taking it off when she came home from Buckingham Palace. Mr Openshaw's face contracted into hard lines; grew like what it was before he had known his wife and her child. He rang the bell, even before his uncle had done speaking. It was answered by the housemaid.

'Mary, was anyone here last night, while we were away?'

'A man, sir, came to speak to Norah.'

'To speak to Norah! Who was he? How long did he stay?'

'I'm sure I can't tell, sir. He came—perhaps about nine. I went up to tell Norah in the nursery, and she came down to speak to him. She let him out, sir. She will know who he was, and how long he stayed.'

She waited a moment to be asked any more questions, but she was not, so she went away.

A minute afterwards Mr Openshaw made as though he were going out of the room; but his wife laid her hand on his arm.

'Do not speak to her before the children,' she said, in her low, quiet voice. 'I will go up and question her.'

'No! I must speak to her. You must know,' said he, turning to his uncle and aunt, 'my missus has an old servant, as faithful as ever woman was, I do believe, as far as love goes,—but at the same time, who does not speak truth, as even the missus must allow. Now, my notion is, that this Norah of ours has been come over by some good-for-nothing chap (for she's at the time o' life when they say women pray for husbands—"any, good Lord, any") and has let him into our house, and the chap has made off with your brooch, and

25

m'appen many another thing beside. It's only saying that Norah is soft-hearted and doesn't stick at a white lie—that's all, missus.'

It was curious to notice how his tone, his eyes, his whole face was changed, as he spoke to his wife; but he was the resolute man through all. She knew better than to oppose him; so she went upstairs, and told Norah that her master wanted to speak to her, and that she would take care of the children in the meanwhile.

Norah rose to go, without a word. Her thoughts were these:

'If they tear me to pieces, they shall never know through me. He may come—and then, just Lord have mercy upon us all! for some of us are dead folk to a certainty. But he shall do it; not me.'

You may fancy, now, her look of determination, as she faced her master alone in the dining-room; Mr and Mrs Chadwick having left the affair in their nephew's hands, seeing that he took it up with such vehemence.

'Norah! Who was that man that came to my house last night?'

'Man, sir!' As if infinitely surprised; but it was only to gain time.

'Yes; the man that Mary let in; that she went upstairs to the nursery to tell you about; that you came down to speak to; the same chap, I make no doubt, that you took into the nursery to have your talk out with; the one Ailsie saw, and afterwards dreamed about; thinking, poor wench! she saw him say his prayers, when nothing, I'll be bound, was further from his thoughts; the one that took Mrs Chadwick's brooch, value ten pounds. Now, Norah! Don't go off. I'm as sure as my name's Thomas Openshaw that you knew nothing of this robbery. But I do think you've been imposed on, and that's the truth. Some good-for-nothing chap has been making up to

26

you, and you've been just like all other women, and have turned a soft place in your heart to him; and he came last night a-lovyering, and you had him up in the nursery, and he made use of his opportunities, and made off with a few things on his way down! Come, now, Norah; it's no blame to you, only you must not be such a fool again! Tell us,' he continued, 'what name he gave you, Norah. I'll be bound, it was not the right one; but it will be a clue for the police.'

Norah drew herself up. 'You may ask that question, and taunt me with my being single, and with my credulity, as you will, Master Openshaw. You'll get no answer from me. As for the brooch, and the story of theft and burglary; if any friend ever came to see me (which I defy you to prove, and deny), he'd be just as much above doing such a thing as you yourself, Mr Openshaw—and more so, too; for I'm not at all sure as everything you have is rightly come by, or would be yours long, if every man had his own.' She meant, of course, his wife; but he understood her to refer to his property in goods and chattels.

'Now, my good woman,' said he, 'I'll just tell you truly, I never trusted you out and out; but my wife liked you, and I thought you had many a good point about you. If you once begin to sauce me, I'll have the police to you, and get out the truth in a court of justice, if you'll not tell it me quietly and civilly here. Now, the best thing you can do is quietly to tell me who the fellow is. Look here! a man comes to my house; asks for you; you take him upstairs; a valuable brooch is missing next day; we know that you, and Mary, and cook, are honest; but you refuse to tell us who the man is. Indeed, you've told me one lie already about him, saying no one was here last night. Now, I just put it to you, what do you think a policeman

27

would say to this, or a magistrate? A magistrate would soon make you tell the truth, my good woman.'

'There's never the creature born that should get it out of me,' said

Norah. 'Not unless I choose to tell.'

'I've a great mind to see,' said Mr Openshaw, growing angry at the defiance. Then, checking himself, he thought before he spoke again:

'Norah, for your missus' sake I don't want to go to extremities. Be a sensible woman, if you can. It's no great disgrace, after all, to have been taken in. I ask you once more — as a friend — who was this man that you let into my house last night?'

No answer. He repeated the question in an impatient tone. Still no answer. Norah's lips were set in determination not to speak.

'Then there is but one thing to be done. I shall send for a policeman.'

'You will not,' said Norah, starting forward. 'You shall not, sir! No policeman shall touch me. I know nothing of the brooch, but I know this: ever since I was four-and-twenty, I have thought more of your wife than of myself: ever since I saw her, a poor motherless girl, put upon in her uncle's house, I have thought more of serving her than of serving myself! I have cared for her and her child, as nobody ever cared for me. I don't cast blame on you, sir, but I say it's ill giving up one's life to anyone; for, at the end, they will turn round upon you, and forsake you. Why does not my missus come herself to suspect me? Maybe, she is gone for the police? But I don't stay here, either for police, or magistrate, or master. You're an unlucky lot. I believe there's a curse on you. I'll leave you this very day. Yes! I'll leave that poor Ailsie, too. I will! No good ever will come to you!'

Mr Openshaw was utterly astonished at this speech; most of which was completely unintelligible to him, as may easily be supposed. Before he could make up his mind what to say, or what to do, Norah had left the room. I do not think he had ever really intended to send for the police to this old servant of his wife's; for he had never for a moment doubted her perfect honesty. But he had intended to compel her to tell him who the man was, and in this he was baffled. He was, consequently, much irritated. He returned to his uncle and aunt in a state of great annoyance and perplexity, and told them he could get nothing out of the woman; that some man had been in the house the night before; but that she refused to tell who he was. At this moment his wife came in, greatly agitated, and asked what had happened to Norah; for that she had put on her things in passionate haste, and left the house.

'This looks suspicious,' said Mr Chadwick. 'It is not the way in which an honest person would have acted.'

Mr Openshaw kept silence. He was sorely perplexed. But Mrs Openshaw turned round on Mr Chadwick, with a sudden fierceness no one ever saw in her before.

'You don't know Norah, uncle! She is gone because she is deeply hurt at being suspected. Oh, I wish I had seen her—that I had spoken to her myself. She would have told me anything.' Alice wrung her hands.

'I must confess,' continued Mr Chadwick to his nephew, in a lower voice, 'I can't make you out. You used to be a word and a blow, and oftenest the blow first; and now, when there is every cause for suspicion, you just do nought. Your missus is a very good woman, I grant; but she may have been put upon as well as other folk, I suppose. If you don't send for the police, I shall.'

'Very well,' replied Mr Openshaw, surlily. 'I can't clear Norah. She won't clear herself, as I believe she might if she would. Only I wash my hands of it; for I am sure the woman herself is honest, and she's lived a long time with my wife, and I don't like her to come to shame.'

'But she will then be forced to clear herself. That, at any rate, will be a good thing.'

'Very well, very well! I am heart-sick of the whole business. Come, Alice, come up to the babies; they'll be in a sore way. I tell you, uncle,' he said, turning round once more to Mr Chadwick, suddenly and sharply, after his eye had fallen on Alice's wan, tearful, anxious face, 'I'll have no sending for the police, after all. I'll buy my aunt twice as handsome a brooch this very day; but I'll not have Norah suspected, and my missus plagued. There's for you!'

He and his wife left the room. Mr Chadwick quietly waited till he was out of hearing, and then said to his wife, 'For all Tom's heroics, I'm just quietly going for a detective, wench. Thou need'st know nought about it.'

He went to the police-station and made a statement of the case. He was gratified by the impression which the evidence against Norah seemed to make. The men all agreed in his opinion, and steps were to be immediately taken to find out where she was. Most probably, as they suggested, she had gone at once to the man, who, to all appearance, was her lover. When Mr Chadwick asked how they would find her out, they smiled, shook their heads, and spoke of mysterious but infallible ways and means. He returned to his nephew's house with a very comfortable opinion of his own sagacity. He was met by his wife with a penitent face.

30

'Oh, master, I've found my brooch! It was just sticking by its pin in the flounce of my brown silk, that I wore yesterday. I took it off in a hurry, and it must have caught in it; and I hung up my gown in the closet. Just now, when I was going to fold it up, there was the brooch! I am very vexed, but I never dreamt but what it was lost!'

Her husband, muttering something very like 'Confound thee and thy brooch too! I wish I'd never given it thee,' snatched up his hat, and rushed back to the station, hoping to be in time to stop the police from searching for Norah. But a detective was already gone off on the errand.

Where was Norah? Half mad with the strain of the fearful secret, she had hardly slept through the night for thinking what must be done. Upon this terrible state of mind had come Ailsie's questions, showing that she had seen the Man, as the unconscious child called her father. Lastly came the suspicion of her honesty. She was little less than crazy as she ran upstairs and dashed on her bonnet and shawl; leaving all else, even her purse, behind her. In that house she would not stay. That was all she knew or was clear about. She would not even see the children again, for fear it should weaken her. She dreaded above everything Mr Frank's return to claim his wife. She could not tell what remedy there was for a sorrow so tremendous, for her to stay to witness. The desire of escaping from the coming event was a stronger motive for her departure, than her soreness about the suspicions directed against her; although this last had been the final goad to the course she took. She walked a way almost at headlong speed; sobbing as she went, as she had not dared to do during the past night for fear of exciting wonder in those who might hear her. Then she stopped. An idea came into her mind that she would leave London altogether, and betake herself to her native town of Liverpool. She felt in her pocket for her purse as

31

she drew near the Euston Square station with this intention. She had left it at home. Her poor head aching, her eyes swollen with crying, she had to stand still, and think, as well as she could, where next she should bend her steps. Suddenly the thought flashed into her mind that she would go and find out poor Mr Frank. She had been hardly kind to him the night before, though her heart had bled for him ever since. She remembered his telling her, when she inquired for his address, almost as she had pushed him out of the door, of some hotel in a street not far distant from Euston Square. Thither she went: with what intention she scarcely knew, but to assuage her conscience by telling him how much she pitied him. In her present state she felt herself unfit to counsel, or restrain, or assist, or do aught else but sympathize and weep. The people of the inn said such a person had been there; had arrived only the day before; had gone out soon after arrival, leaving his luggage in their care; but had never come back. Norah asked for leave to sit down, and await the gentleman's return. The landlady—pretty secure in the deposit of luggage against any probable injury—showed her into a room, and quietly locked the door on the outside. Norah was utterly worn out, and fell asleep—a shivering, starting, uneasy slumber, which lasted for hours.

The detective, meanwhile, had come up with her some time before she entered the hotel, into which he followed her. Asking the landlady to detain her for an hour or so, without giving any reason beyond showing his authority (which made the landlady applaud herself a good deal for having locked her in), he went back to the police-station to report his proceedings. He could have taken her directly; but his object was, if possible, to trace out the man who was supposed to have committed the robbery. Then he heard of the discovery of the brooch; and consequently did not care to return.

32

Norah slept till even the summer evening began to close in, Then started up. Someone was at the door. It would be Mr Frank; and she dizzily pushed back her ruffled grey hair which had fallen over her eyes, and stood looking to see him. Instead, there came in Mr Openshaw and a policeman.

'This is Norah Kennedy,' said Mr Openshaw.

'Oh, sir,' said Norah, 'I did not touch the brooch; indeed I did not. Oh, sir, I cannot live to be thought so badly of'; and very sick and faint, she suddenly sank down on the ground. To her surprise, Mr Openshaw raised her up very tenderly. Even the policeman helped to lay her on the sofa; and, at Mr Openshaw's desire, he went for some wine and sandwiches; for the poor gaunt woman lay there almost as if dead with weariness and exhaustion.

'Norah,' said Mr Openshaw, in his kindest voice, 'the brooch is found. It was hanging to Mrs Chadwick's gown. I beg your pardon. Most truly I beg your pardon, for having troubled you about it. My wife is almost broken-hearted. Eat, Norah—or, stay, first drink this glass of wine,' said he, lifting her head, and pouring a little down her throat.

As she drank, she remembered where she was, and who she was waiting for. She suddenly pushed Mr Openshaw away, saying, 'Oh, sir, you must go. You must not stop a minute. If he comes back, he will kill you.'

'Alas, Norah! I do not know who "he" is. But someone is gone away who will never come back: someone who knew you, and whom I am afraid you cared for.'

'I don't understand you, sir,' said Norah, her master's kind and sorrowful manner bewildering her yet more than his words. The policeman had left the room at Mr Openshaw's desire, and they two were alone.

'You know what I mean, when I say someone is gone who will never come back. I mean that he is dead!'

'Who?' said Norah, trembling all over.

'A poor man has been found in the Thames this morning—drowned.'

'Did he drown himself?' asked Norah, solemnly.

'God only knows,' replied Mr Openshaw, in the same tone. 'Your name and address at our house were found in his pocket; that, and his purse, were the only things that were found upon him. I am sorry to say it, my poor Norah; but you are required to go and identify him.'

'To what?' asked Norah.

'To say who it is. It is always done, in order that some reason may be discovered for the suicide—if suicide it was. I make no doubt, he was the man who came to see you at our house last night. It is very sad, I know.' He made pauses between each little clause, in order to try and bring back her senses, which he feared were wandering—so wild and sad was her look.

'Master Openshaw,' said she, at last, 'I've a dreadful secret to tell you—only you must never breathe it to anyone, and you and I must hide it away for ever. I thought to have done it all by myself, but I see I cannot. Yon poor man—yes! the dead, drowned creature is, I fear, Mr Frank, my mistress's first husband!'

34

Mr Openshaw sat down, as if shot. He did not speak; but, after a while, he signed to Norah to go on.

'He came to me the other night, when—God be thanked!—you were all away at Richmond. He asked me if his wife was dead or alive. I was a brute, and thought more of your all coming home than of his sore trial; I spoke out sharp, and said she was married again, and very content and happy. I all but turned him away: and now he lies dead and cold.'

'God forgive me!' said Mr Openshaw.

'God forgive us all!' said Norah. 'Yon poor man needs forgiveness, perhaps, less than any one among us. He had been among the savages—shipwrecked—I know not what—and he had written letters which had never reached my poor missus.'

'He saw his child!'

'He saw her—yes! I took him up, to give his thoughts another start; for I believed he was going mad on my hands. I came to seek him here, as I more than half promised. My mind misgave me when I heard he never came in. Oh, sir, it must be him!'

Mr Openshaw rang the bell. Norah was almost too much stunned to wonder at what he did. He asked for writing materials, wrote a letter, and then said to Norah:

'I am writing to Alice, to say I shall be unavoidably absent for a few days; that I have found you; that you are well, and send her your love, and will come home tomorrow. You must go with me to the police court; you must identify the body; I will pay high to keep names and details out of the papers.'

35

'But where are you going, sir?'

He did not answer her directly. Then he said:

'Norah! I must go with you, and look on the face of the man whom I have so injured—unwittingly, it is true; but it seems to me as if I had killed him. I will lay his head in the grave as if he were my only brother: and how he must have hated me! I cannot go home to my wife till all that I can do for him is done. Then I go with a dreadful secret on my mind. I shall never speak of it again, after these days are over. I know you will not, either.' He shook hands with her; and they never named the subject again, the one to the other.

Norah went home to Alice the next day. Not a word was said on the cause of her abrupt departure a day or two before. Alice had been charged by her husband, in his letter, not to allude to the supposed theft of the brooch; so she, implicitly obedient to those whom she loved both by nature and habit, was entirely silent on the subject, only treated Norah with the most tender respect, as if to make up for unjust suspicion.

Nor did Alice inquire into the reason why Mr Openshaw had been absent during his uncle and aunt's visit, after he had once said that it was unavoidable. He came back grave and quiet; and from that time forth was curiously changed. More thoughtful, and perhaps less active; quite as decided in conduct, but with new and different rules for the guidance of that conduct. Towards Alice he could hardly be more kind than he had always been; but he now seemed to look upon her as someone sacred, and to be treated with reverence, as well as tenderness. He throve in business, and made a large fortune, one half of which was settled upon her.

Long years after these events—a few months after her mother

died—Ailsie and her 'father' (as she always called Mr Openshaw) drove to a cemetery a little way out of town, and she was carried to a certain mound by her maid, who was then sent back to the carriage. There was a headstone, with F.W. and a date upon it. That was all. Sitting by the grave, Mr Openshaw told her the story; and for the sad fate of that poor father whom she had never seen, he shed the only tears she ever saw fall from his eyes.

# THOMAS HARDY

# A MERE INTERLUDE

## (The Bolton Weekly Journal, 17 and 24 October 1885)

# I

The traveller in school-books, who vouched in dryest tones for the fidelity to fact of the following narrative, used to add a ring of truth to it by opening with a nicety of criticism on the heroine's personality. People were wrong, he declared, when they surmised that Baptista Trewthen was a young woman with scarcely emotions or character. There was nothing in her to love, and nothing to hate—so ran the general opinion. That she showed few positive qualities was true. The colours and tones which changing events paint on the faces of active womankind were looked for in vain upon hers. But still waters run deep; and no crisis had come in the years of her early maidenhood to demonstrate what lay hidden within her, like metal in a mine.

She was the daughter of a small farmer in St Maria's, one of the Isles of Lyonesse beyond Off-Wessex, who had spent a large sum, as there understood, on her education, by sending her to the mainland for two years. At nineteen she was entered at the Training College for Teachers, and at twenty-one nominated to a school in the country, near Tor-upon-Sea, whither she proceeded after the Christmas examination and holidays.

The months passed by from winter to spring and summer, and Baptista applied herself to her new duties as best she could, till an uneventful year had elapsed. Then an air of abstraction pervaded her bearing as she walked to and fro, twice a day, and she showed the traits of a person who had something on her mind. A widow, by name Mrs Wace, in whose house Baptista Trewthen had been provided with a sitting-room and bedroom till the schoolhouse should be built, noticed this change in her youthful tenant's manner, and at last ventured to press her with a few questions.

'It has nothing to do with the place, nor with you,' said Miss Trewthen.

'Then it is the salary?'

'No, nor the salary.'

'Then it is something you have heard from home, my dear.'

Baptista was silent for a few moments. 'It is Mr Heddegan,' she murmured. 'Him they used to call David Heddegan before he got his money.'

'And who is the Mr Heddegan they used to call David?'

'An old bachelor at Giant's Town, St Maria's, with no relations whatever, who lives about a stone's throw from father's. When I was a child he used to take me on his knee and say he'd marry me some day. Now I am a woman the jest has turned earnest, and he is anxious to do it. And father and mother say I can't do better than have him.'

39

'He's well off?'

'Yes—he's the richest man we know—as a friend and neighbour.'

'How much older did you say he was than yourself?'

'I didn't say. Twenty years at least.'

'And an unpleasant man in the bargain perhaps?'

'No—he's not unpleasant.'

'Well, child, all I can say is that I'd resist any such engagement if it's not palatable to 'ee. You are comfortable here, in my little house, I hope. All the parish like 'ee: and I've never been so cheerful, since my poor husband left me to wear his wings, as I've been with 'ee as my lodger.'

The schoolmistress assured her landlady that she could return the sentiment. 'But here comes my perplexity,' she said. 'I don't like keeping school. Ah, you are surprised—you didn't suspect it. That's because I've concealed my feeling. Well, I simply hate school. I don't care for children—they are unpleasant, troublesome little things, whom nothing would delight so much as to hear that you had fallen down dead. Yet I would even put up with them if it was not for the inspector. For three months before his visit I didn't sleep soundly. And the Committee of Council are always changing the Code, so that you don't know what to teach, and what to leave untaught. I think father and mother are right. They say I shall never excel as a schoolmistress if I dislike the work so, and that therefore I ought to get settled by marrying Mr Heddegan. Between us two, I like him better than school; but I don't like him quite so much as to wish to marry him.'

These conversations, once begun, were continued from day to day; till at length the young girl's elderly friend and landlady threw in her opinion on the side of Miss Trewthen's parents. All things considered, she declared, the uncertainty of the school, the labour, Baptista's natural dislike for teaching, it would be as well to take what fate offered, and make the best of matters by wedding her father's old neighbour and prosperous friend.

The Easter holidays came round, and Baptista went to spend them as usual in her native isle, going by train into Off-Wessex and crossing by packet from Pen-zephyr. When she returned in the middle of April her face wore a more settled aspect.

'Well?' said the expectant Mrs Wace.

'I have agreed to have him as my husband,' said Baptista, in an off-hand way. 'Heaven knows if it will be for the best or not. But I have agreed to do it, and so the matter is settled.'

Mrs Wace commended her; but Baptista did not care to dwell on the subject; so that allusion to it was very infrequent between them. Nevertheless, among other things, she repeated to the widow from time to time in monosyllabic remarks that the wedding was really impending; that it was arranged for the summer, and that she had given notice of leaving the school at the August holidays. Later on she announced more specifically that her marriage was to take place immediately after her return home at the beginning of the month aforesaid.

She now corresponded regularly with Mr Heddegan. Her letters from him were seen, at least on the outside, and in part within, by Mrs Wace. Had she read more of their interiors than the occasional sentences shown her by Baptista she would have perceived that the

41

scratchy, rusty handwriting of Miss Trewthen's betrothed conveyed little more matter than details of their future housekeeping, and his preparations for the same, with innumerable 'my dears' sprinkled in disconnectedly, to show the depth of his affection without the inconveniences of syntax.

## II

It was the end of July—dry, too dry, even for the season, the delicate green herbs and vegetables that grew in this favoured end of the kingdom tasting rather of the watering-pot than of the pure fresh moisture from the skies. Baptista's boxes were packed, and one Saturday morning she departed by a waggonette to the station, and thence by train to Pen-zephyr, from which port she was, as usual, to cross the water immediately to her home, and become Mr Heddegan's wife on the Wednesday of the week following.

She might have returned a week sooner. But though the wedding day had loomed so near, and the banns were out, she delayed her departure till this last moment, saying it was not necessary for her to be at home long beforehand. As Mr Heddegan was older than herself, she said, she was to be married in her ordinary summer bonnet and grey silk frock, and there were no preparations to make that had not been amply made by her parents and intended husband.

In due time, after a hot and tedious journey, she reached Pen-zephyr. She here obtained some refreshment, and then went towards the pier, where she learnt to her surprise that the little steamboat plying between the town and the islands had left at eleven o'clock; the usual hour of departure in the afternoon having

42

been forestalled in consequence of the fogs which had for a few days prevailed towards evening, making twilight navigation dangerous.

This being Saturday, there was now no other boat till Tuesday, and it became obvious that here she would have to remain for the three days, unless her friends should think fit to rig out one of the island sailing-boats and come to fetch her—a not very likely contingency, the sea distance being nearly forty miles.

Baptista, however, had been detained in Pen-zephyr on more than one occasion before, either on account of bad weather or some such reason as the present, and she was therefore not in any personal alarm. But, as she was to be married on the following Wednesday, the delay was certainly inconvenient to a more than ordinary degree, since it would leave less than a day's interval between her arrival and the wedding ceremony.

Apart from this awkwardness she did not much mind the accident. It was indeed curious to see how little she minded. Perhaps it would not be too much to say that, although she was going to do the critical deed of her life quite willingly, she experienced an indefinable relief at the postponement of her meeting with Heddegan. But her manner after making discovery of the hindrance was quiet and subdued, even to passivity itself; as was instanced by her having, at the moment of receiving information that the steamer had sailed, replied 'Oh', so coolly to the porter with her luggage, that he was almost disappointed at her lack of disappointment.

The question now was, should she return again to Mrs Wace, in the village of Lower Wessex, or wait in the town at which she had arrived. She would have preferred to go back, but the distance was too great; moreover, having left the place for good, and somewhat dramatically, to become a bride, a return, even for so short a space, would have been a trifle humiliating.

Leaving, then, her boxes at the station, her next anxiety was to secure a respectable, or rather genteel, lodging in the popular seaside resort confronting her. To this end she looked about the town, in which, though she had passed through it half-a-dozen times, she was practically a stranger.

Baptista found a room to suit her over a fruiterer's shop; where she made herself at home, and set herself in order after her journey. An early cup of tea having revived her spirits she walked out to reconnoitre.

Being a schoolmistress she avoided looking at the schools, and having a sort of trade connection with books, she avoided looking at the booksellers; but wearying of the other shops she inspected the churches; not that for her own part she cared much about ecclesiastical edifices; but tourists looked at them, and so would she—a proceeding for which no one would have credited her with any great originality, such, for instance, as that she subsequently showed herself to possess. The churches soon oppressed her. She tried the Museum, but came out because it seemed lonely and tedious.

Yet the town and the walks in this land of strawberries, these headquarters of early English flowers and fruit, were then, as always, attractive. From the more picturesque streets she went to the town gardens, and the Pier, and the Harbour, and looked at the men at work there, loading and unloading as in the time of the Phoenicians.

44

'Not Baptista? Yes, Baptista it is!'

The words were uttered behind her. Turning round she gave a start, and became confused, even agitated, for a moment. Then she said in her usual undemonstrative manner, 'O—is it really you, Charles?'

Without speaking again at once, and with a half-smile, the newcomer glanced her over. There was much criticism, and some resentment—even temper—in his eye.

'I am going home,' continued she. 'But I have missed the boat.'

He scarcely seemed to take in the meaning of this explanation, in the intensity of his critical survey. 'Teaching still? What a fine schoolmistress you make, Baptista, I warrant!' he said with a slight flavour of sarcasm, which was not lost upon her.

'I know I am nothing to brag of,' she replied. 'That's why I have given up.'

'O—given up? You astonish me.'

'I hate the profession.'

'Perhaps that's because I am in it.'

'O no, it isn't. But I am going to enter on another life altogether. I am going to be married next week to Mr David Heddegan.'

The young man—fortified as he was by a natural cynical pride and passionateness—winced at this unexpected reply, notwithstanding.

'Who is Mr David Heddegan?' he asked, as indifferently as lay in his power.

She informed him the bearer of the name was a general merchant of

45

Giant's Town, St Maria's Island—her father's nearest neighbour and oldest friend.

'Then we shan't see anything more of you on the mainland?' inquired the schoolmaster.

'O, I don't know about that,' said Miss Trewthen.

'Here endeth the career of the belle of the boarding-school your father was foolish enough to send you to. A "general merchant's" wife in the Lyonesse Isles. Will you sell pounds of soap and pennyworths of tin tacks, or whole bars of saponaceous matter, and great tenpenny nails?'

'He's not in such a small way as that!' she almost pleaded. 'He owns ships, though they are rather little ones!'

'O, well, it is much the same. Come, let us walk on; it is tedious to stand still. I thought you would be a failure in education,' he continued, when she obeyed him and strolled ahead. 'You never showed power that way. You remind me much of some of those women who think they are sure to be great actresses if they go on the stage, because they have a pretty face, and forget that what we require is acting. But you found your mistake, didn't you?'

'Don't taunt me, Charles.' It was noticeable that the young schoolmaster's tone caused her no anger or retaliatory passion; far otherwise: there was a tear in her eye. 'How is it you are at Penzephyr?' she inquired.

'I don't taunt you. I speak the truth, purely in a friendly way, as I should to anyone I wished well. Though for that matter I might have some excuse even for taunting you. Such a terrible hurry as you've been in. I hate a woman who is in such a hurry.'

46

'How do you mean that?'

'Why—to be somebody's wife or other—anything's wife rather than nobody's. You couldn't wait for me, O, no. Well, thank God, I'm cured of all that!'

'How merciless you are!' she said bitterly. 'Wait for you? What does that mean, Charley? You never showed—anything to wait for—anything special towards me.'

'O come, Baptista dear; come!'

'What I mean is, nothing definite,' she expostulated. 'I suppose you liked me a little; but it seemed to me to be only a pastime on your part, and that you never meant to make an honourable engagement of it.'

'There, that's just it! You girls expect a man to mean business at the first look. No man when he first becomes interested in a woman has any definite scheme of engagement to marry her in his mind, unless he is meaning a vulgar mercenary marriage. However, I did at last mean an honourable engagement, as you call it, come to that.'

'But you never said so, and an indefinite courtship soon injures a woman's position and credit, sooner than you think.'

'Baptista, I solemnly declare that in six months I should have asked you to marry me.'

She walked along in silence, looking on the ground, and appearing very uncomfortable. Presently he said, 'Would you have waited for me if you had known?' To this she whispered in a sorrowful whisper, 'Yes!'

They went still farther in silence—passing along one of the

47

beautiful walks on the outskirts of the town, yet not observant of scene or situation. Her shoulder and his were close together, and he clasped his fingers round the small of her arm—quite lightly, and without any attempt at impetus; yet the act seemed to say, 'Now I hold you, and my will must be yours.'

Recurring to a previous question of hers he said, 'I have merely run down here for a day or two from school near Trufal, before going off to the north for the rest of my holiday. I have seen my relations at Redrutin quite lately, so I am not going there this time. How little I thought of meeting you! How very different the circumstances would have been if, instead of parting again as we must in half-an-hour or so, possibly for ever, you had been now just going off with me, as my wife, on our honeymoon trip. Ha—ha—well—so humorous is life!'

She stopped suddenly. 'I must go back now—this is altogether too painful, Charley! It is not at all a kind mood you are in today.'

'I don't want to pain you—you know I do not,' he said more gently. 'Only it just exasperates me—this you are going to do. I wish you would not.'

'What?'

'Marry him. There, now I have showed you my true sentiments.'

'I must do it now,' said she.

'Why?' he asked, dropping the off-hand masterful tone he had hitherto spoken in, and becoming earnest; still holding her arm, however, as if she were his chattel to be taken up or put down at will. 'It is never too late to break off a marriage that's distasteful to

48

you. Now I'll say one thing; and it is truth: I wish you would marry me instead of him, even now, at the last moment, though you have served me so badly.'

'O, it is not possible to think of that!' she answered hastily, shaking her head. 'When I get home all will be prepared—it is ready even now—the things for the party, the furniture, Mr. Heddegan's new suit, and everything. I should require the courage of a tropical lion to go home there and say I wouldn't carry out my promise!'

'Then go, in Heaven's name! But there would be no necessity for you to go home and face them in that way. If we were to marry, it would have to be at once, instantly; or not at all. I should think your affection not worth the having unless you agreed to come back with me to Trufal this evening, where we could be married by licence on Monday morning. And then no Mr. David Heddegan or anybody else could get you away from me.'

'I must go home by the Tuesday boat,' she faltered. 'What would they think if I did not come?'

'You could go home by that boat just the same. All the difference would be that I should go with you. You could leave me on the quay, where I'd have a smoke, while you went and saw your father and mother privately; you could then tell them what you had done, and that I was waiting not far off; that I was a schoolmaster in a fairly good position, and a young man you had known when you were at the Training College. Then I would come boldly forward; and they would see that it could not be altered, and so you wouldn't suffer a lifelong misery by being the wife of a wretched old gaffer you don't like at all. Now, honestly; you do like me best, don't you, Baptista?'

49

'Yes.'

'Then we will do as I say.'

She did not pronounce a clear affirmative. But that she consented to the novel proposition at some moment or other of that walk was apparent by what occurred a little later.

# III

An enterprise of such pith required, indeed, less talking than consideration. The first thing they did in carrying it out was to return to the railway station, where Baptista took from her luggage a small trunk of immediate necessaries which she would in any case have required after missing the boat. That same afternoon they travelled up the line to Trufal.

Charles Stow (as his name was), despite his disdainful indifference to things, was very careful of appearances, and made the journey independently of her though in the same train. He told her where she could get board and lodgings in the city; and with merely a distant nod to her of a provisional kind, went off to his own quarters, and to see about the licence.

On Sunday she saw him in the morning across the nave of the pro-cathedral. In the afternoon they walked together in the fields, where he told her that the licence would be ready next day, and would be available the day after, when the ceremony could be performed as early after eight o'clock as they should choose.

His courtship, thus renewed after an interval of two years, was as impetuous, violent even, as it was short. The next day came and

50

passed, and the final arrangements were made. Their agreement was to get the ceremony over as soon as they possibly could the next morning, so as to go on to Pen-zephyr at once, and reach that place in time for the boat's departure the same day. It was in obedience to Baptista's earnest request that Stow consented thus to make the whole journey to Lyonesse by land and water at one heat, and not break it at Pen-zephyr; she seemed to be oppressed with a dread of lingering anywhere, this great first act of disobedience to her parents once accomplished, with the weight on her mind that her home had to be convulsed by the disclosure of it. To face her difficulties over the water immediately she had created them was, however, a course more desired by Baptista than by her lover; though for once he gave way.

The next morning was bright and warm as those which had preceded it. By six o'clock it seemed nearly noon, as is often the case in that part of England in the summer season. By nine they were husband and wife. They packed up and departed by the earliest train after the service; and on the way discussed at length what she should say on meeting her parents, Charley dictating the turn of each phrase. In her anxiety they had travelled so early that when they reached Pen-zephyr they found there were nearly two hours on their hands before the steamer's time of sailing.

Baptista was extremely reluctant to be seen promenading the streets of the watering-place with her husband till, as above stated, the household at Giant's Town should know the unexpected course of events from her own lips; and it was just possible, if not likely, that some Lyonessian might be prowling about there, or even have come across the sea to look for her. To meet anyone to whom she was known, and to have to reply to awkward questions about the

51

strange young man at her side before her well-framed announcement had been delivered at proper time and place, was a thing she could not contemplate with equanimity. So, instead of looking at the shops and harbour, they went along the coast a little way.

The heat of the morning was by this time intense. They clambered up on some cliffs, and while sitting there, looking around at St Michael's Mount and other objects, Charles said to her that he thought he would run down to the beach at their feet, and take just one plunge into the sea.

Baptista did not much like the idea of being left alone; it was gloomy, she said. But he assured her he would not be gone more than a quarter of an hour at the outside, and she passively assented.

Down he went, disappeared, appeared again, and looked back. Then he again proceeded, and vanished, till, as a small waxen object, she saw him emerge from the nook that had screened him, cross the white fringe of foam, and walk into the undulating mass of blue. Once in the water he seemed less inclined to hurry than before; he remained a long time; and, unable either to appreciate his skill or criticize his want of it at that distance, she withdrew her eyes from the spot, and gazed at the still outline of St Michael's— now beautifully toned in grey.

Her anxiety for the hour of departure, and to cope at once with the approaching incidents that she would have to manipulate as best she could, sent her into a reverie. It was now Tuesday; she would reach home in the evening—a very late time they would say; but, as the delay was a pure accident, they would deem her marriage to Mr Heddegan tomorrow still practicable. Then Charles would have to be produced from the background. It was a terrible undertaking to think of, and she almost regretted her temerity in wedding so hastily that morning. The rage of her father would be so crushing; the reproaches of her mother so bitter; and perhaps Charles would answer hotly, and perhaps cause estrangement till death. There had obviously been no alarm about her at St Maria's, or somebody would have sailed across to inquire for her. She had, in a letter written at the beginning of the week, spoken of the hour at which she intended to leave her country schoolhouse; and from this her friends had probably perceived that by such timing she would run a risk of losing the Saturday boat. She had missed it, and as a consequence sat here on the shore as Mrs Charles Stow.

This brought her to the present, and she turned from the outline of St Michael's Mount to look about for her husband's form. He was, as far as she could discover, no longer in the sea. Then he was dressing. By moving a few steps she could see where his clothes lay. But Charles was not beside them.

Baptista looked back again at the water in bewilderment, as if her senses were the victim of some sleight of hand. Not a speck or spot resembling a man's head or face showed anywhere. By this time she was alarmed, and her alarm intensified when she perceived a little beyond the scene of her husband's bathing a small area of water, the quality of whose surface differed from that of the surrounding expanse as the coarse vegetation of some foul patch in a mead differs from the fine green of the remainder. Elsewhere it looked flexuous, here it looked vermiculated and lumpy, and her marine experiences suggested to her in a moment that two currents met and caused a turmoil at this place.

She descended as hastily as her trembling limbs would allow. The

53

way down was terribly long, and before reaching the heap of clothes it occurred to her that, after all, it would be best to run first for help. Hastening along in a lateral direction she proceeded inland till she met a man, and soon afterwards two others. To them she exclaimed, 'I think a gentleman who was bathing is in some danger. I cannot see him as I could. Will you please run and help him, at once, if you will be so kind?'

She did not think of turning to show them the exact spot, indicating it vaguely by the direction of her hand, and still going on her way with the idea of gaining more assistance. When she deemed, in her faintness, that she had carried the alarm far enough, she faced about and dragged herself back again. Before reaching the now dreaded spot she met one of the men.

'We can see nothing at all, Miss,' he declared.

Having gained the beach, she found the tide in, and no sign of Charley's clothes. The other men whom she had besought to come had disappeared, it must have been in some other direction, for she had not met them going away. They, finding nothing, had probably thought her alarm a mere conjecture, and given up the quest.

Baptista sank down upon the stones near at hand. Where Charley had undressed was now sea. There could not be the least doubt that he was drowned, and his body sucked under by the current; while his clothes, lying within high-water mark, had probably been carried away by the rising tide.

She remained in a stupor for some minutes, till a strange sensation succeeded the aforesaid perceptions, mystifying her intelligence, and leaving her physically almost inert. With his personal

54

disappearance, the last three days of her life with him seemed to be swallowed up, also his image, in her mind's eye, waned curiously, receded far away, grew stranger and stranger, less and less real. Their meeting and marriage had been so sudden, unpremeditated, adventurous, that she could hardly believe that she had played her part in such a reckless drama. Of all the few hours of her life with Charles, the portion that most insisted in coming back to memory was their fortuitous encounter on the previous Saturday, and those bitter reprimands with which he had begun the attack, as it might be called, which had piqued her to an unexpected consummation.

A sort of cruelty, an imperiousness, even in his warmth, had characterized Charles Stow. As a lover he had ever been a bit of a tyrant; and it might pretty truly have been said that he had stung her into marriage with him at last. Still more alien from her life did these reflections operate to make him; and then they would be chased away by an interval of passionate weeping and mad regret. Finally, there returned upon the confused mind of the young wife the recollection that she was on her way homeward, and that the packet would sail in three-quarters of an hour.

Except the parasol in her hand, all she possessed was at the station awaiting her onward journey.

She looked in that direction; and, entering one of those undemonstrative phases so common with her, walked quietly on.

At first she made straight for the railway; but suddenly turning she went to a shop and wrote an anonymous line announcing his death by drowning to the only person she had ever heard Charles mention as a relative. Posting this stealthily, and with a fearful look around her, she seemed to acquire a terror of the late events, pursuing her way to the station as if followed by a spectre.

When she got to the office she asked for the luggage that she had left there on the Saturday as well as the trunk left on the morning just lapsed. All were put in the boat, and she herself followed. Quickly as these things had been done, the whole proceeding, nevertheless, had been almost automatic on Baptista's part, ere she had come to any definite conclusion on her course.

Just before the bell rang she heard a conversation on the pier, which removed the last shade of doubt from her mind, if any had existed, that she was Charles Stow's widow. The sentences were but fragmentary, but she could easily piece them out.

'A man drowned—swam out too far—was a stranger to the place—people in boat—saw him go down—couldn't get there in time.'

The news was little more definite than this as yet; though it may as well be stated once for all that the statement was true. Charley, with the over-confidence of his nature, had ventured out too far for his strength, and succumbed in the absence of assistance, his lifeless body being at the moment suspended in the transparent mid-depths of the bay. His clothes, however, had merely been gently lifted by the rising tide, and floated into a nook hard by, where they lay out of sight of the passers-by till a day or two after.

## IV

In ten minutes they were steaming out of the harbour for their voyage of four or five hours, at whose ending she would have to tell her strange story.

As Pen-zephyr and all its environing scenes disappeared behind Mousehole and St Clement's Isle, Baptista's ephemeral, meteor-like

56

husband impressed her yet more as a fantasy. She was still in such a trance-like state that she had been an hour on the little packet-boat before she became aware of the agitating fact that Mr Heddegan was on board with her. Involuntarily she slipped from her left hand the symbol of her wifehood.

'Hee-hee! Well, the truth is, I wouldn't interrupt 'ee. "I reckon she don't see me, or won't see me," I said, "and what's the hurry? She'll see enough o' me soon!" I hope ye be well, mee deer?'

He was a hale, well-conditioned man of about five and fifty, of the complexion common to those whose lives are passed on the bluffs and beaches of an ocean isle. He extended the four quarters of his face in a genial smile, and his hand for a grasp of the same magnitude. She gave her own in surprised docility, and he continued:

'I couldn't help coming across to meet 'ee. What an unfortunate thing you missing the boat and not coming Saturday! They meant to have warned 'ee that the time was changed, but forgot it at the last moment. The truth is that I should have informed 'ee myself, but I was that busy finishing up a job last week, so as to have this week free, that I trusted to your father for attending to these little things. However, so plain and quiet as it is all to be, it really do not matter so much as it might otherwise have done, and I hope ye haven't been greatly put out. Now, if you'd sooner that I should not be seen talking to 'ee—if 'ee feel shy at all before strangers—just say. I'll leave 'ee to yourself till we get home.'

'Thank you much. I am indeed a little tired, Mr Heddegan.'

He nodded urbane acquiescence, strolled away immediately, and minutely inspected the surface of the funnel, till some female passengers of Giant's Town tittered at what they must have thought a rebuff—for the approaching wedding was known to many on St Maria's Island, though to nobody elsewhere. Baptista coloured at their satire, and called him back, and forced herself to commune with him in at least a mechanically friendly manner.

The opening event had been thus different from her expectation, and she had adumbrated no act to meet it. Taken aback she passively allowed circumstances to pilot her along; and so the voyage was made.

It was near dusk when they touched the pier of Giant's Town, where several friends and neighbours stood awaiting them. Her father had a lantern in his hand. Her mother, too, was there, reproachfully glad that the delay had at last ended so simply. Mrs Trewthen and her daughter went together along the Giant's Walk, or promenade, to the house, rather in advance of her husband and Mr Heddegan, who talked in loud tones which reached the women over their shoulders.

Some would have called Mrs Trewthen a good mother; but though well meaning she was maladroit, and her intentions missed their mark. This might have been partly attributable to the slight deafness from which she suffered. Now, as usual, the chief utterances came from her lips.

'Ah, yes, I'm so glad, my child, that you've got over safe. It is all ready, and everything so well arranged, that nothing but misfortune could hinder you settling as, with God's grace, becomes 'ee. Close to your mother's door a'most, 'twill be a great blessing, I'm sure; and I was very glad to find from your letters that you'd held your word sacred. That's right—make your word your bond always. Mrs Wace seems to be a sensible woman. I hope the Lord will do for her as he's doing for you no long time hence. And how did 'ee get over the terrible journey from Tor-upon-Sea to Penzephyr? Once you'd done with the railway, of course, you seemed quite at home. Well, Baptista, conduct yourself seemly, and all will be well.'

Thus admonished, Baptista entered the house, her father and Mr Heddegan immediately at her back. Her mother had been so didactic that she had felt herself absolutely unable to broach the subjects in the centre of her mind.

The familiar room, with the dark ceiling, the well-spread table, the old chairs, had never before spoken so eloquently of the times ere she knew or had heard of Charley Stow. She went upstairs to take off her things, her mother remaining below to complete the disposition of the supper, and attend to the preparation of tomorrow's meal, altogether composing such an array of pies, from pies of fish to pies of turnips, as was never heard of outside the Western Duchy. Baptista, once alone, sat down and did nothing; and was called before she had taken off her bonnet.

'I'm coming,' she cried, jumping up, and speedily disapparelling herself, brushed her hair with a few touches and went down.

Two or three of Mr Heddegan's and her father's friends had dropped in, and expressed their sympathy for the delay she had been subjected to. The meal was a most merry one except to Baptista. She had desired privacy, and there was none; and to break the news was already a greater difficulty than it had been at first. Everything around her, animate and inanimate, great and small, insisted that she had come home to be married; and she could not get a chance to say nay.

One or two people sang songs, as overtures to the melody of the morrow, till at length bedtime came, and they all withdrew, her mother having retired a little earlier. When Baptista found herself again alone in her bedroom the case stood as before: she had come home with much to say, and she had said nothing.

It was now growing clear even to herself that Charles being dead, she had not determination sufficient within her to break tidings which, had he been alive, would have imperatively announced themselves. And thus with the stroke of midnight came the turning of the scale; her story should remain untold. It was not that upon the whole she thought it best not to attempt to tell it; but that she could not undertake so explosive a matter. To stop the wedding now would cause a convulsion in Giant's Town little short of volcanic. Weakened, tired, and terrified as she had been by the day's adventures, she could not make herself the author of such a catastrophe. But how refuse Heddegan without telling? It really seemed to her as if her marriage with Mr Heddegan were about to take place as if nothing had intervened.

Morning came. The events of the previous days were cut off from her present existence by scene and sentiment more completely than ever. Charles Stow had grown to be a special being of whom, owing to his character, she entertained rather fearful than loving memory. Baptista could hear when she awoke that her parents were already moving about downstairs. But she did not rise till her mother's rather rough voice resounded up the staircase as it had done on the preceding evening.

'Baptista! Come, time to be stirring! The man will be here, by Heaven's blessing, in three-quarters of an hour. He has looked in already for a minute or two—and says he's going to the church to see if things be well forward.'

Baptista arose, looked out of the window, and took the easy course. When she emerged from the regions above she was arrayed in her new silk frock and best stockings, wearing a linen jacket over the former for breakfasting, and her common slippers over the latter, not to spoil the new ones on the rough precincts of the dwelling.

It is unnecessary to dwell at any great length on this part of the morning's proceedings. She revealed nothing; and married Heddegan, as she had given her word to do, on that appointed August day.

## V

Mr Heddegan forgave the coldness of his bride's manner during and after the wedding ceremony, full well aware that there had been considerable reluctance on her part to acquiesce in this neighbourly arrangement, and, as a philosopher of long standing, holding that whatever Baptista's attitude now, the conditions would probably be much the same six months hence as those which ruled among other married couples.

An absolutely unexpected shock was given to Baptista's listless mind about an hour after the wedding service. They had nearly finished the midday dinner when the now husband said to her father, 'We think of starting about two. And the breeze being so fair we shall bring up inside Pen-zephyr new pier about six at least.'

'What—are we going to Pen-zephyr?' said Baptista. 'I don't know anything of it.'

'Didn't you tell her?' asked her father of Heddegan.

It transpired that, owing to the delay in her arrival, this proposal too, among other things, had in the hurry not been mentioned to her, except some time ago as a general suggestion that they would go somewhere. Heddegan had imagined that any trip would be pleasant, and one to the mainland the pleasantest of all.

She looked so distressed at the announcement that her husband willingly offered to give it up, though he had not had a holiday off the island for a whole year. Then she pondered on the inconvenience of staying at Giant's Town, where all the inhabitants were bonded, by the circumstances of their situation, into a sort of family party, which permitted and encouraged on such occasions as these oral criticism that was apt to disturb the equanimity of newly married girls, and would especially worry Baptista in her strange situation. Hence, unexpectedly, she agreed not to disorganize her husband's plans for the wedding jaunt, and it was settled that, as originally intended, they should proceed in a neighbour's sailing boat to the metropolis of the district.

In this way they arrived at Pen-zephyr without difficulty or mishap. Bidding adieu to Jenkin and his man, who had sailed them over, they strolled arm in arm off the pier, Baptista silent, cold, and obedient. Heddegan had arranged to take her as far as Plymouth before their return, but to go no further than where they had landed that day. Their first business was to find an inn; and in this they had unexpected difficulty, since for some reason or other—possibly the fine weather—many of the nearest at hand were full of tourists and commercial travellers. He led her on till he reached a tavern which, though comparatively unpretending, stood in as attractive a spot as any in the town; and this, somewhat to their surprise after their previous experience, they found apparently empty. The considerate old man, thinking that Baptista was educated to artistic notions, though he himself was deficient in them, had decided that it was most desirable to have, on such an occasion as the present, an apartment with 'a good view' (the expression being one he had often heard in use among tourists); and he therefore asked for a favourite room on the first floor, from which a bow-window protruded, for the express purpose of affording such an outlook.

The landlady, after some hesitation, said she was sorry that particular apartment was engaged; the next one, however, or any other in the house, was unoccupied.

'The gentleman who has the best one will give it up tomorrow, and then you can change into it,' she added, as Mr Heddegan hesitated about taking the adjoining and less commanding one.

'We shall be gone tomorrow, and shan't want it,' he said.

Wishing not to lose customers, the landlady earnestly continued that since he was bent on having the best room, perhaps the other gentleman would not object to move at once into the one they despised, since, though nothing could be seen from the window, the room was equally large.

'Well, if he doesn't care for a view,' said Mr Heddegan, with the air of a highly artistic man who did.

'O no—I am sure he doesn't,' she said. 'I can promise that you shall have the room you want. If you would not object to go for a walk for half an hour, I could have it ready, and your things in it, and a nice tea laid in the bow-window by the time you come back?'

This proposal was deemed satisfactory by the fussy old tradesman, and they went out. Baptista nervously conducted him in an opposite direction to her walk of the former day in other company, showing on her wan face, had he observed it, how much she was beginning to regret her sacrificial step for mending matters that morning.

She took advantage of a moment when her husband's back was turned to inquire casually in a shop if anything had been heard of the gentleman who was sucked down in the eddy while bathing.

The shopman said, 'Yes, his body has been washed ashore,' and had just handed Baptista a newspaper on which she discerned the heading, 'A Schoolmaster drowned while bathing', when her husband turned to join her. She might have pursued the subject without raising suspicion; but it was more than flesh and blood could do, and completing a small purchase almost ran out of the shop.

'What is your terrible hurry, mee deer?' said Heddegan, hastening after.

'I don't know—I don't want to stay in shops,' she gasped.

'And we won't,' he said. 'They are suffocating this weather. Let's go back and have some tay!'

They found the much desired apartment awaiting their entry. It was a sort of combination bed and sitting-room, and the table was prettily spread with high tea in the bow-window, a bunch of flowers in the midst, and a best-parlour chair on each side. Here they shared the meal by the ruddy light of the vanishing sun. But though the view had been engaged, regardless of expense, exclusively for Baptista's pleasure, she did not direct any keen attention out of the window. Her gaze as often fell on the floor and walls of the room as elsewhere, and on the table as much as on either, beholding nothing at all.

But there was a change. Opposite her seat was the door, upon which her eyes presently became riveted like those of a little bird upon a snake. For, on a peg at the back of the door, there hung a hat; such a hat—surely, from its peculiar make, the actual hat—that had been worn by Charles. Conviction grew to certainty when she saw a railway ticket sticking up from the band. Charles had put the ticket there—she had noticed the act.

Her teeth almost chattered; she murmured something incoherent. Her husband jumped up and said, 'You are not well! What is it? What shall I get 'ee?'

'Smelling salts!' she said, quickly and desperately; 'at the chemist's shop you were in just now.'

He jumped up like the anxious old man that he was, caught up his own hat from a back table, and without observing the other hastened out and downstairs.

Left alone she gazed and gazed at the back of the door, then spasmodically rang the bell. An honest-looking country maid-servant appeared in response.

'A hat!' murmured Baptista, pointing with her finger. 'It does not belong to us.'

'O yes, I'll take it away,' said the young woman with some hurry 'It belongs to the other gentleman.'

She spoke with a certain awkwardness, and took the hat out of the room. Baptista had recovered her outward composure. 'The other gentleman?' she said. 'Where is the other gentleman?'

'He's in the next room, ma'am. He removed out of this to oblige 'ee.'

'How can you say so? I should hear him if he were there,' said Baptista, sufficiently recovered to argue down an apparent untruth.

'He's there,' said the girl, hardily.

'Then it is strange that he makes no noise,' said Mrs Heddegan, convicting the girl of falsity by a look.

'He makes no noise; but it is not strange,' said the servant.

All at once a dread took possession of the bride's heart, like a cold hand laid thereon; for it flashed upon her that there was a possibility of reconciling the girl's statement with her own knowledge of facts.

'Why does he make no noise?' she weakly said.

The waiting-maid was silent, and looked at her questioner. 'If I tell you, ma'am, you won't tell missis?' she whispered.

Baptista promised.

'Because he's a-lying dead!' said the girl. 'He's the schoolmaster that was drowned yesterday.'

'O!' said the bride, covering her eyes. 'Then he was in this room till just now?'

'Yes,' said the maid, thinking the young lady's agitation natural enough. 'And I told missis that I thought she oughtn't to have done it, because I don't hold it right to keep visitors so much in the dark

66

where death's concerned; but she said the gentleman didn't die of anything infectious; she was a poor, honest, innkeeper's wife, she says, who had to get her living by making hay while the sun sheened. And owing to the drowned gentleman being brought here, she said, it kept so many people away that we were empty, though all the other houses were full. So when your good man set his mind upon the room, and she would have lost good paying folk if he'd not had it, it wasn't to be supposed, she said, that she'd let anything stand in the way. Ye won't say that I've told ye, please, m'm? All the linen has been changed, and as the inquest won't be till tomorrow, after you are gone, she thought you wouldn't know a word of it, being strangers here.'

The returning footsteps of her husband broke off further narration. Baptista waved her hand, for she could not speak. The waiting-maid quickly withdrew, and Mr Heddegan entered with the smelling salts and other nostrums.

'Any better?' he questioned.

'I don't like the hotel,' she exclaimed, almost simultaneously. 'I can't bear it—it doesn't suit me!'

'Is that all that's the matter?' he returned pettishly (this being the first time of his showing such a mood). 'Upon my heart and life such trifling is trying to any man's temper, Baptista! Sending me about from here to yond, and then when I come back saying 'ee don't like the place that I have sunk so much money and words to get for 'ee. 'Od dang it all, 'tis enough to—But I won't say any more at present, mee deer, though it is just too much to expect to turn out of the house now. We shan't get another quiet place at this time of the evening—every other inn in the town is bustling with rackety

67

folk of one sort and t'other, while here 'tis as quiet as the grave—the country, I would say. So bide still, d'ye hear, and tomorrow we shall be out of the town altogether—as early as you like.'

The obstinacy of age had, in short, overmastered its complaisance, and the young woman said no more. The simple course of telling him that in the adjoining room lay a corpse which had lately occupied their own might, it would have seemed, have been an effectual one without further disclosure, but to allude to that subject, however it was disguised, was more than Heddegan's young wife had strength for. Horror broke her down. In the contingency one thing only presented itself to her paralysed regard—that here she was doomed to abide, in a hideous contiguity to the dead husband and the living, and her conjecture did, in fact, bear itself out. That night she lay between the two men she had married—Heddegan on the one hand, and on the other through the partition against which the bed stood, Charles Stow.

# VI

Kindly time had withdrawn the foregoing event three days from the present of Baptista Heddegan. It was ten o'clock in the morning; she had been ill, not in an ordinary or definite sense, but in a state of cold stupefaction, from which it was difficult to arouse her so much as to say a few sentences. When questioned she had replied that she was pretty well.

Their trip, as such, had been something of a failure. They had gone on as far as Falmouth, but here he had given way to her entreaties to return home. This they could not very well do without repassing through Pen-zephyr, at which place they had now again arrived.

68

In the train she had seen a weekly local paper, and read there a paragraph detailing the inquest on Charles. It was added that the funeral was to take place at his native town of Redrutin on Friday.

After reading this she had shown no reluctance to enter the fatal neighbourhood of the tragedy, only stipulating that they should take their rest at a different lodging from the first; and now comparatively braced up and calm—indeed a cooler creature altogether than when last in the town, she said to David that she wanted to walk out for a while, as they had plenty of time on their hands.

'To a shop as usual, I suppose, mee deer?'

'Partly for shopping,' she said. 'And it will be best for you, dear, to stay in after trotting about so much, and have a good rest while I am gone.'

He assented; and Baptista sallied forth. As she had stated, her first visit was made to a shop, a draper's. Without the exercise of much choice she purchased a black bonnet and veil, also a black stuff gown; a black mantle she already wore. These articles were made up into a parcel which, in spite of the saleswoman's offers, her customer said she would take with her. Bearing it on her arm she turned to the railway, and at the station got a ticket for Redrutin.

Thus it appeared that, on her recovery from the paralysed mood of the former day, while she had resolved not to blast utterly the happiness of her present husband by revealing the history of the departed one, she had also determined to indulge a certain odd, inconsequent, feminine sentiment of decency, to the small extent to which it could do no harm to any person. At Redrutin she emerged from the railway carnage in the black attire purchased at the shop,

69

having during the transit made the change in the empty compartment she had chosen. The other clothes were now in the bandbox and parcel. Leaving these at the cloak-room she proceeded onward, and after a wary survey reached the side of a hill whence a view of the burial ground could be obtained.

It was now a little before two o'clock. While Baptista waited a funeral procession ascended the road. Baptista hastened across, and by the time the procession entered the cemetery gates she had unobtrusively joined it.

In addition to the schoolmaster's own relatives (not a few), the paragraph in the newspapers of his death by drowning had drawn together many neighbours, acquaintances, and onlookers.

Among them she passed unnoticed, and with a quiet step pursued the winding path to the chapel, and afterwards thence to the grave. When all was over, and the relatives and idlers had withdrawn, she stepped to the edge of the chasm. From beneath her mantle she drew a little bunch of forget-me-nots, and dropped them in upon the coffin. In a few minutes she also turned and went away from the cemetery. By five o'clock she was again in Pen-zephyr.

'You have been a mortal long time!' said her husband, crossly. 'I allowed you an hour at most, mee deer.'

'It occupied me longer,' said she.

'Well—I reckon it is wasting words to complain. Hang it, ye look so tired and wisht that I can't find heart to say what I would!'

'I am—weary and wisht, David; I am. We can get home tomorrow for certain, I hope?'

70

'We can. And please God we will!' said Mr Heddegan heartily, as if he too were weary of his brief honeymoon. 'I must be into business again on Monday morning at latest.'

They left by the next morning steamer, and in the afternoon took up their residence in their own house at Giant's Town.

The hour that she reached the island it was as if a material weight had been removed from Baptista's shoulders. Her husband attributed the change to the influence of the local breezes after the hot-house atmosphere of the mainland. However that might be, settled here, a few doors from her mother's dwelling, she recovered in no very long time much of her customary bearing, which was never very demonstrative. She accepted her position calmly, and faintly smiled when her neighbours learned to call her Mrs Heddegan, and said she seemed likely to become the leader of fashion in Giant's Town.

Her husband was a man who had made considerably more money by trade than her father had done: and perhaps the greater profusion of surroundings at her command than she had heretofore been mistress of, was not without an effect upon her. One week, two weeks, three weeks passed; and, being pre-eminently a young woman who allowed things to drift, she did nothing whatever either to disclose or conceal traces of her first marriage; or to learn if there existed possibilities—which there undoubtedly did—by which that hasty contract might become revealed to those about her at any unexpected moment.

While yet within the first month of her marriage, and on an evening just before sunset, Baptista was standing within her garden adjoining the house, when she saw passing along the road a personage clad in a greasy black coat and battered tall hat, which, common enough in the slums of a city, had an odd appearance in St Maria's. The tramp, as he seemed to be, marked her at once—bonnetless and unwrapped as she was her features were plainly recognizable—and with an air of friendly surprise came and leant over the wall.

'What! don't you know me?' said he.

She had some dim recollection of his face, but said that she was not acquainted with him.

'Why, your witness to be sure, ma'am. Don't you mind the man that was mending the church-window when you and your intended husband walked up to be made one; and the clerk called me down from the ladder, and I came and did my part by writing my name and occupation?'

Baptista glanced quickly around; her husband was out of earshot. That would have been of less importance but for the fact that the wedding witnessed by this personage had not been the wedding with Mr. Heddegan, but the one on the day previous.

'I've had a misfortune since then, that's pulled me under,' continued her friend. 'But don't let me damp yer wedded joy by naming the particulars. Yes, I've seen changes since; though 'tis but a short time ago—let me see, only a month next week, I think; for 'twere the first or second day in August.'

'Yes—that's when it was,' said another man, a sailor, who had come up with a pipe in his mouth, and felt it necessary to join in (Baptista having receded to escape further speech). 'For that was the first time I set foot in Giant's Town; and her husband took her to him the same day.'

A dialogue then proceeded between the two men outside the wall, which Baptista could not help hearing.

'Ay, I signed the book that made her one flesh,' repeated the decayed glazier. 'Where's her good-man?'

'About the premises somewhere; but you don't see'em together much,' replied the sailor in an undertone. 'You see, he's older than she.'

'Older? I should never have thought it from my own observation,' said the glazier. 'He was a remarkably handsome man.'

'Handsome? Well, there he is—we can see for ourselves.'

David Heddegan had, indeed, just shown himself at the upper end of the garden; and the glazier, looking in bewilderment from the husband to the wife, saw the latter turn pale.

Now that decayed glazier was a far-seeing and cunning man—too far-seeing and cunning to allow himself to thrive by simple and straightforward means—and he held his peace, till he could read more plainly the meaning of this riddle, merely added carelessly, 'Well—marriage do alter a man, 'tis true. I should never ha' knowed him!'

He then stared oddly at the disconcerted Baptista, and moving on to where he could again address her, asked her to do him a good turn, since he once had done the same for her. Understanding that he meant money, she handed him some, at which he thanked her, and instantly went away.

# VII

She had escaped exposure on this occasion; but the incident had been an awkward one, and should have suggested to Baptista that sooner or later the secret must leak out. As it was, she suspected that at any rate she had not heard the last of the glazier.

In a day or two, when her husband had gone to the old town on the other side of the island, there came a gentle tap at the door, and the worthy witness of her first marriage made his appearance a second time.

'It took me hours to get to the bottom of the mystery—hours!' he said with a gaze of deep confederacy which offended her pride very deeply. 'But thanks to a good intellect I've done it. Now, ma'am, I'm not a man to tell tales, even when a tale would be so good as this. But I'm going back to the mainland again, and a little assistance would be as rain on thirsty ground.'

'I helped you two days ago,' began Baptista.

'Yes—but what was that, my good lady? Not enough to pay my passage to Pen-zephyr. I came over on your account, for I thought there was a mystery somewhere. Now I must go back on my own. Mind this—'twould be very awkward for you if your old man were to know. He's a queer temper, though he may be fond.'

She knew as well as her visitor how awkward it would be; and the hush-money she paid was heavy that day. She had, however, the satisfaction of watching the man to the steamer, and seeing him diminish out of sight. But Baptista perceived that the system into which she had been led of purchasing silence thus was one fatal to her peace of mind, particularly if it had to be continued.

Hearing no more from the glazier she hoped the difficulty was past. But another week only had gone by, when, as she was pacing the Giant's Walk (the name given to the promenade), she met the same personage in the company of a fat woman carrying a bundle.

'This is the lady, my dear,' he said to his companion. 'This, ma'am, is my wife. We've come to settle in the town for a time, if so be we can find room.'

'That you won't do,' said she. 'Nobody can live here who is not privileged.'

'I am privileged,' said the glazier, 'by my trade.'

Baptista went on, but in the afternoon she received a visit from the man's wife. This honest woman began to depict, in forcible colours, the necessity for keeping up the concealment.

'I will intercede with my husband, ma'am,' she said. 'He's a true man if rightly managed; and I'll beg him to consider your position. 'Tis a very nice house you've got here,' she added, glancing round, 'and well worth a little sacrifice to keep it.'

The unlucky Baptista staved off the danger on this third occasion as she had done on the previous two. But she formed a resolve that, if the attack were once more to be repeated she would face a revelation—worse though that must now be than before she had attempted to purchase silence by bribes. Her tormentors, never believing her capable of acting upon such an intention, came again; but she shut the door in their faces. They retreated, muttering something; but she went to the back of the house, where David Heddegan was.

She looked at him, unconscious of all. The case was serious; she knew that well; and all the more serious in that she liked him better now than she had done at first. Yet, as she herself began to see, the secret was one that was sure to disclose itself. Her name and Charles's stood indelibly written in the registers; and though a month only had passed as yet it was a wonder that his clandestine union with her had not already been discovered by his friends. Thus spurring herself to the inevitable, she spoke to Heddegan.

'David, come indoors. I have something to tell you.'

He hardly regarded her at first. She had discerned that during the last week or two he had seemed preoccupied, as if some private business harassed him. She repeated her request. He replied with a sigh, 'Yes, certainly, mee deer.'

When they had reached the sitting-room and shut the door she repeated, faintly, 'David, I have something to tell you—a sort of tragedy I have concealed. You will hate me for having so far deceived you; but perhaps my telling you voluntarily will make you think a little better of me than you would do otherwise.'

'Tragedy?' he said, awakening to interest. 'Much you can know about tragedies, mee deer, that have been in the world so short a time!'

She saw that he suspected nothing, and it made her task the harder. But on she went steadily. 'It is about something that happened before we were married,' she said.

'Indeed!'

'Not a very long time before—a short time. And it is about a lover,' she faltered.

76

'I don't much mind that,' he said mildly. 'In truth, I was in hopes 'twas more.'

'In hopes!'

'Well, yes.'

This screwed her up to the necessary effort. 'I met my old sweetheart. He scorned me, chid me, dared me, and I went and married him. We were coming straight here to tell you all what we had done; but he was drowned; and I thought I would say nothing about him: and I married you, David, for the sake of peace and quietness. I've tried to keep it from you, but have found I cannot. There—that's the substance of it, and you can never, never forgive me, I am sure!'

She spoke desperately. But the old man, instead of turning black or blue, or slaying her in his indignation, jumped up from his chair, and began to caper around the room in quite an ecstatic emotion.

'O, happy thing! How well it falls out!' he exclaimed, snapping his fingers over his head. 'Ha-ha—the knot is cut—I see a way out of my trouble—ha-ha!'

She looked at him without uttering a sound, till, as he still continued smiling joyfully, she said, 'O—what do you mean? Is it done to torment me?'

'No—no! O, mee deer, your story helps me out of the most heart-aching quandary a poor man ever found himself in! You see, it is this—I've got a tragedy, too; and unless you had had one to tell, I could never have seen my way to tell mine!'

77

'What is yours—what is it?' she asked, with altogether a new view of things.

'Well—it is a bouncer; mine is a bouncer!' said he, looking on the ground and wiping his eyes.

'Not worse than mine?'

'Well—that depends upon how you look at it. Yours had to do with the past alone; and I don't mind it. You see, we've been married a month, and it don't jar upon me as it would if we'd only been married a day or two. Now mine refers to past, present, and future; so that—'

'Past, present, and future!' she murmured. 'It never occurred to me that you had a tragedy too.'

'But I have!' he said, shaking his head. 'In fact, four.'

'Then tell 'em!' cried the young woman.

'I will—I will. But be considerate, I beg 'ee, mee deer. Well—I wasn't a bachelor when I married 'ee, any more than you were a spinster. Just as you was a widow-woman, I was a widow-man.'

'Ah!' said she, with some surprise. 'But is that all?—then we are nicely balanced,' she added, relieved.

'No—it is not all. There's the point. I am not only a widower.'

'O, David!'

'I am a widower with four tragedies—that is to say, four strapping girls—the eldest taller than you. Don't 'ee look so struck—dumb-like! It fell out in this way. I knew the poor woman, their mother, in

78

Pen-zephyr for some years; and—to cut a long story short—I privately married her at last, just before she died. I kept the matter secret, but it is getting known among the people here by degrees. I've long felt for the children—that it is my duty to have them here, and do something for them. I have not had courage to break it to 'ee, but I've seen lately that it would soon come to your ears, and that hev worried me.'

'Are they educated?' said the ex-schoolmistress.

'No. I am sorry to say they have been much neglected; in truth, they can hardly read. And so I thought that by marrying a young schoolmistress I should get some one in the house who could teach 'em, and bring 'em into genteel condition, all for nothing. You see, they are growed up too tall to be sent to school.'

'O, mercy!' she almost moaned. 'Four great girls to teach the rudiments to, and have always in the house with me spelling over their books; and I hate teaching, it kills me. I am bitterly punished— I am, I am!'

'You'll get used to 'em, mee deer, and the balance of secrets—mine against yours—will comfort your heart with a sense of justice. I could send for 'em this week very well—and I will! In faith, I could send this very day. Baptista, you have relieved me of all my difficulty!'

Thus the interview ended, so far as this matter was concerned. Baptista was too stupefied to say more, and when she went away to her room she wept from very mortification at Mr Heddegan's duplicity. Education, the one thing she abhorred; the shame of it to delude a young wife so!

The next meal came round. As they sat, Baptista would not suffer her eyes to turn towards him. He did not attempt to intrude upon her reserve, but every now and then looked under the table and chuckled with satisfaction at the aspect of affairs. 'How very well matched we be!' he said, comfortably.

Next day, when the steamer came in, Baptista saw her husband rush down to meet it; and soon after there appeared at her door four tall, hipless, shoulderless girls, dwindling in height and size from the eldest to the youngest, like a row of Pan pipes; at the head of them standing Heddegan. He smiled pleasantly through the grey fringe of his whiskers and beard, and turning to the girls said, 'Now come forrard, and shake hands properly with your stepmother.'

Thus she made their acquaintance, and he went out, leaving them together. On examination the poor girls turned out to be not only plain-looking, which she could have forgiven, but to have such a lamentably meagre intellectual equipment as to be hopelessly inadequate as companions. Even the eldest, almost her own age, could only read with difficulty words of two syllables; and taste in dress was beyond their comprehension. In the long vista of future years she saw nothing but dreary drudgery at her detested old trade without prospect of reward.

She went about quite despairing during the next few days—an unpromising, unfortunate mood for a woman who had not been married six weeks. From her parents she concealed everything. They had been amongst the few acquaintances of Heddegan who knew nothing of his secret, and were indignant enough when they saw such a ready-made household foisted upon their only child. But she would not support them in their remonstrances.

'No, you don't yet know all,' she said.

80

Thus Baptista had sense enough to see the retributive fairness of this issue. For some time, whenever conversation arose between her and Heddegan, which was not often, she always said, 'I am miserable, and you know it. Yet I don't wish things to be otherwise.'

But one day when he asked, 'How do you like 'em now?' her answer was unexpected. 'Much better than I did,' she said, quietly. 'I may like them very much some day.'

This was the beginning of a serener season for the chastened spirit of Baptista Heddegan. She had, in truth, discovered, underneath the crust of uncouthness and meagre articulation which was due to their Troglodytean existence, that her unwelcomed daughters had natures that were unselfish almost to sublimity. The harsh discipline accorded to their young lives before their mother's wrong had been righted, had operated less to crush them than to lift them above all personal ambition. They considered the world and its contents in a purely objective way, and their own lot seemed only to affect them as that of certain human beings among the rest, whose troubles they knew rather than suffered.

This was such an entirely new way of regarding life to a woman of Baptista's nature, that her attention, from being first arrested by it, became deeply interested. By imperceptible pulses her heart expanded in sympathy with theirs. The sentences of her tragi-comedy, her life, confused till now, became clearer daily. That in humanity, as exemplified by these girls, there was nothing to dislike, but infinitely much to pity, she learnt with the lapse of each week in their company. She grew to like the girls of unpromising exterior, and from liking she got to love them; till they formed an unexpected point of junction between her own and her husband's interests, generating a sterling friendship at least, between a pair in

81

whose existence there had threatened to be neither friendship nor
love.

# GEORGE MOORE

# A FAITHFUL HEART

## (The Speaker, 16 April 1892)

## Part I

It was a lovely morning, and Major Shepherd walked rapidly, his toes turned well out, his shoulders set well back. Behind him floated the summer foliage of Appleton Park—the family seat of the Shepherds—and at the end of the smooth, white road lay the Major's destination—the small town of Branbury.

The Major was the medium height; his features were regular and cleanly cut. He would have been a handsome man if his eyes had not been two dark mud-coloured dots, set close together, wholly lacking in expression. A long brown moustache swept picturesquely over bright, smoothly shaven cheeks, and the ends of this ornament were beginning to whiten. The Major was over forty. He carried under his arm a brown-paper parcel (the Major was rarely seen without a brown-paper parcel), and in it were things he could not possibly do without—his diary and his letter-book. The brown-paper parcel contained likewise a number of other papers; it contained the Major's notes for a book he was writing on the principal county families in Buckinghamshire. The Major had been

83

collecting information for this book for many years, and with it he hoped to make two or three hundred pounds—money which he stood sorely in need of—and to advance his position in the county, a position which, in his opinion, his father had done little to maintain, and which, to his very deep regret, his sisters were now doing their best to compromise. That very morning, while packing up his brown-paper parcel, some quarter of an hour ago, he had had a somewhat angry interview on this subject with his sisters. For he had thought it his duty to reprove them for keeping company with certain small London folk who had chosen to come to live in the neighbourhood. Ethel had said that they were not going to give up their friends because they were not good enough for him, and Maud had added significantly that they were quite sure that their friends were quite as good as the friend he was going to see in Branbury. The Major turned on his heel and left the house.

As he walked towards Branbury he asked himself if it were possible that they knew anything about Charlotte Street; and as he approached the town he looked round nervously, fearing lest some friend might pop down upon him, and, after some hesitation, decided to take a long detour so as to avoid passing by the house of some people he knew. As he made his way through a bye-street his step quickened, and at the corner of Charlotte Street he looked round to make sure he was not followed. He then drew his keys from his pocket and let himself into a small, mean-looking house.

Major Shepherd might have spared himself the trouble of these precautions; no one was minded to watch him, for everyone knew perfectly well who lived in 27, Charlotte Street. It was common talk that the tall, dark woman who lived in 27 was Mrs Charles Shepherd, and that the little girl who ran by Mrs Shepherd's side on the rare occasions when she was seen in the streets—for it was said that the Major did not wish her to walk much about the town, lest she should attract the attention of the curious, who might be tempted to make inquiries—was the Major's little daughter, and it had been noticed that this little girl went forth now and then, basket on her arm, to do the marketing. It was said that Mrs Shepherd had been a servant in some lodging-house where the Major had been staying; other scandal-mongers declared that they knew for certain that the Major had made his wife's acquaintance in the street. Rumour had never wandered far from the truth. The Major had met his wife one night as he was coming home from his club. They seemed to suit one another; he saw her frequently for several months, and then, fearing to lose her, in a sudden access of jealousy—he had some time before been bitterly jilted—he proposed to marry her. The arrival of his parents, who came up to town beseeching of him to do nothing rash, only served to intensify his determination, and, losing his temper utterly, he told his father and mother that he would never set his foot in Appleton Park in their lifetime if they ever again ventured to pry into his private affairs; and, refusing to give any information regarding his intentions, he asked them to leave his lodgings. What he did after they never knew; years went by, and they sighed and wondered, but the matter was never alluded to in Appleton Park.

But the Major had only £400 a year, and though he lived at Appleton Park, never spending a penny more than was necessary, he could not allow her more than £3 a week. He had so many expenses: his club, his clothes, and all the incidental expenses he was put to in the grand houses where he went to stay. By strict economy, however, Mrs Shepherd managed to make two ends meet. Except when she was too ill and had to call in a charwoman to help her with the heaviest part of the work, she undertook the entire housework herself: when times were hardest, she had even taken in a lodger, not thinking herself above cooking and taking up his dinner. She had noticed that her economies endeared her to the Major, and it was pleasant to please him. Hers was a kind-hearted, simple nature, that misfortune had brought down in the world; but, as is not uncommon with persons of weak character, she possessed a clear, sensible mind which allowed her to see things in their true lights, and without difficulty she recognized the unalterable nature of her case. It mattered little whether the Major acknowledged her or not, his family would never have anything to do with her; the doors of Society were for ever closed against her. So within a year of her marriage with the Major she was convinced that her marriage had better be kept a secret; for, by helping to keep it a secret, she could make substantial amends to the man who had married her; by proclaiming it to the world, she would only alienate his affection. She understood this very well, and in all docility and obedience lent herself to the deception, accepting without complaint a mean and clandestine existence. But she would not allow her little girl to carry up a jug of hot water, and it was only rarely, when prostrate with pain, that she allowed Nellie to take the basket and run round to the butcher's and buy a bit of steak for their dinner. The heiress of Appleton Park must be brought up free from all degrading memory. But for herself she had no care. Appleton Park could never be anything to her, even if she outlived the old people, which was hardly probable. What would she, a poor invalid, do there? She did not wish to compromise her husband's future, and still less the future of her darling daughter. She could only hope that, when dead, her sins would be forgiven her; and that this release might not be long delayed she often prayed. The house was poor, and she was miserable, but any place was good enough to suffer in. So she said when she rose and dragged herself downstairs to do a little cooking; and the same thought came to her when she lay all alone in the little parlour, furnished with what a few pounds could buy—a paraffin-lamp, a round table, a few chairs, an old and ill-padded mahogany armchair, in which it was a torture to lie; not an ornament on the chimney-piece, not a flower, not a book to while away the interminable hours. From the barren little passage, covered with a bit of oil-cloth, all and everything in 27 was meagre and unimaginative. The Major had impressed his personality upon the house. Everything looked as if it had been scraped. There was a time when Mrs Shepherd noticed the barrenness of her life; but she had grown accustomed to it, and she waited for the Major in the terrible armchair, glad when she heard his step, almost happy when he sat by her and told her what was happening 'at home'.

He took her hand and asked her how she was. 'You are looking very tired, Alice.'

'Yes, I'm a little tired. I have been working all the morning. I made up my room, and then I went out to the butcher's and bought a piece of steak. I have made you such a nice pudding for your lunch; I hope you will like it.'

'There's not much fear about my liking any beefsteak pudding you make, dear; I never knew anyone who could make one like you. But you should not tire yourself—and just as you are beginning to get better.'

Mrs Shepherd smiled and pressed her husband's hand. The conversation fell. At the end of a long silence Mrs Shepherd said:

'What has happened to trouble you, dear? I know something has, I can see it by your face.'

Then the Major told how unpleasantly his sisters had answered him when he had ventured to suggest that they saw far too much of their new neighbours, who were merely common sort of Londoners, and never would be received by the county. 'I'm sure that someone must have told them of my visits here; I'm sure they suspect something ... Girls are very sharp nowadays.'

'I am sorry, but it is no fault of mine. I rarely leave the house, and I never walk in the principal streets if I can possibly help it.'

'I know, dear, I know that no one can be more careful than you; but as people are beginning to smell a rat notwithstanding all our precautions, I suppose there's nothing for it but to go back to London.'

'Oh, you don't think it will be necessary to go back to London, do you? The place suits the child so well, and it is so nice to see you almost every day; and it is such a comfort when you are not here to know you are only a few miles away; and from the top of the hill the trees of the park are visible, and whenever I feel well enough I walk there and think of the time our Nellie will be the mistress of all those broad acres.'

'It is the fault of the busybodies,' he said; 'I cannot think what pleasure people find in meddling in other people's affairs. I never care what anyone else does. I have quite enough to do thinking of my own.'

Mrs Shepherd did not answer. 'I see,' he said, 'you don't like moving, but if you remain here all the trouble we have taken not to get found out these last ten years will go for nothing. There will be more worry and vexations, and I really don't think I could bear much more; I believe I should go off my head.' The little man spoke in a calm, even voice, and stroked his silky moustache gravely.

'Very well, then, my dear, I'll return to town as soon as you like—as soon as it is convenient. I daresay you are right.'

'I'm sure I am. You have never found me giving you wrong advice yet, have you, dear?'

Then they went down to the kitchen to eat the steak pudding; and when the Major had finished his second helping he lit his pipe, and the conversation turned on how they should get rid of their house, and how much the furniture would fetch. When he had decided to sell the furniture, and had fixed the day of their departure, Mrs Shepherd said—

'There's one thing I have to ask you, dear, and I hope you won't refuse my request. I should like to see Appleton Park before I leave. I should like to go there with Nellie and see the house and the lands that will one day belong to her.'

'I don't know how it is to be managed. If you were to meet my mother and sisters they would be sure to suspect something at once.'

'No one will know who I am. I should like to walk about the grounds for half an hour with the child. If I don't see Appleton now I never shall see it.'

The Major stroked his long, silky moustache with his short, crabbed little hand. He remembered that he had heard the carriage ordered for two o'clock—they were all going to a tennis-party some miles distant. Under the circumstances she might walk about the grounds without being noticed. He did not think any of the gardeners would question her, and, if they did, he could trust her to give an evasive answer. And then he would like her to see the place—just to know what she thought of it.

'Won't you say yes?' she said at last, her voice breaking the silence sharply.

'I was just thinking, dear: they have all gone to a tennis-party today. There'll be no one at home.'

'Well! why not today?'

'Well; I was thinking I've been lucky enough to get hold of some very interesting information about the Websters—about their ancestor Sir Thomas, who distinguished himself in the Peninsular—and I wanted to get it copied under the proper heading, but I daresay we can do that another day. The only thing is, how are you to get there? You are not equal to walking so far—'

'I was thinking, dear, that I might take a fly. I know there is the expense, but ...'

'Yes; five or six shillings, at least. And where will you leave the fly? At the lodge gate? The flyman would be sure to get into conversation with the lodge-keeper or his wife. He'd tell them where he came from, and—'

'Supposing you were to get a two-wheeled trap and drive me yourself; that would be nicer still.'

'I'm so unlucky; someone would be sure to see me.'

The Major puffed at his pipe in silence. Then he said, 'If you were to put on a thick veil, and we were to get out of the town by this end and make our way through the lanes—it would be a long way round; but one hardly meets anyone that way, and the only danger would be going. We should return in the dusk. I don't care how late you make it; my people won't be home till nine or ten o'clock at night, perhaps later still. There will be dancing, and they are sure to stay late.'

Finally the matter was decided, and about four o'clock the Major went to the livery stable to order the trap. Mrs Shepherd and Nellie joined him soon after. Turning from the pony, whose nose he was stroking, he said—

'I hope you have brought a thick shawl; it will be cold coming back in the evening.'

'Yes, dear, here it is, and another for Nellie. What do you think of this veil?'

'It will do very well. I do hope these stablemen won't talk; let's go off at once.' The Major lifted in the child, tucked the rug about them, and cried to the stableman to let go. He drove very nervously, afraid at every moment lest the pony should bolt; and when the animal's extreme docility assured him there was no such danger, he looked round right and left, expecting at every moment some friend to pounce down upon him. But the ways were empty, the breeze that came across the fields was fresh and sweet, and they were all beginning to enjoy themselves, when he suddenly espied a carriage following in his wake. He whipped up the pony, and contrived to distance his imaginary pursuer; and having succeeded, he praised his own driving, and at the cross-roads he said: 'I dare

91

not go any farther, but you can't miss the lodge gate in that clump of trees—the first white gate you come to. Don't ask any questions; it is ten to one you'll find the gate open; walk straight through, and don't forget to go through the beech-wood at the back of the house; the river runs right round the hill. I want to know what you think of the view. But pray don't ask to see the house; there's nothing to see; the housemaids would be sure to talk, and describe you to my sisters. So now goodbye; hope you'll enjoy yourself. I shall have just time to get to Hambrook and back; I want to see my solicitor. You'll have seen everything in a couple of hours, so in a couple of hours I shall be waiting for you here.'

## Part II

It was as the Major said. The lodge-keepers asked no questions, and they passed up the drive, through the silence of an overgrowth of laurels and rhododendrons. Then the park opened before their eyes. Nellie rolled on the short, crisp, worn grass, or chased the dragonflies; the spreading trees enchanted her, and, looking at the house—a grey stone building with steps, pillars, and pilasters, hidden amid cedars and evergreen oaks—she said, 'I never saw anything so beautiful; is that where the Major goes when he leaves us? Look at the flowers, Mother, and the roses. May we not go in there—I don't mean into the house? I heard the Major ask you not to go in for fear we should meet the housemaids—but just past this railing, into the garden? Here is the gate.' The child stood with her hand on the wicket, waiting for reply: the mother stood as in a dream, looking at the house, thinking vaguely of the pictures, the corridors, and staircases, that lay behind the plate-glass windows.

'Yes; go in, my child.'

The gardens were in tumult of leaf and bloom, and the little girl ran hither and thither, gathering single flowers, and then everything that came under her hands, binding them together in bouquets— one for mother, one for the Major, and one for herself. Mrs Shepherd only smiled a little bitterly when Nellie came running to her with some new and more splendid rose. She did not attempt to reprove the child. Why should she? Everything here would one day be hers. Why then should the present be denied them? And so did her thoughts run as she walked across the sward following Nellie into the beech wood that clothed the steep hillside. The pathway led by the ruins of some Danish military earthworks, ancient hollows full of leaves and silence. Pigeons cooed in the vast green foliage, and from time to time there came up from the river the chiming sound of oars. Rustic seats were at pleasant intervals, and, feeling a little tired, Mrs Shepherd sat down. She could see the river's silver glinting through the branches, and, beyond the river, the low-lying river lands, dotted with cattle and horses grazing, dim already with blue evening vapours. In the warm solitude of the wood the irreparable misfortune of her own life pressed upon her: and in this hour of lassitude her loneliness seemed more than she could bear. The Major was good and kind, but he knew nothing of the weight of the burden he had laid upon her, and that none should know was in this moment a greater weight than the burden itself. Nellie was exploring the ancient hollows where Danes and Saxons had once fought, and had ceased to call forth her discoveries when Mrs Shepherd's bitter meditation was broken by the sudden sound of a footstep.

The intruder was a young lady. She was dressed in white, her pale gold hair was in itself an aristocracy, and her narrow slippered feet were dainty to look upon. 'Don't let me disturb you,' she said. 'This is my favourite seat; but I pray you not to move, there is plenty of room.' So amiable was she in voice and manner that Mrs Shepherd could not but remain, although she had already recognized the girl as one of the Major's sisters. Fearing to betray herself, greatly nervous, Mrs Shepherd answered briefly Miss Shepherd's allusions to the beauty of the view. At the end of a long silence Miss Shepherd said—

'I think you know my brother, Major Shepherd.'

Mrs Shepherd hesitated, and then she said: 'No. I have never heard the name.'

'Are you sure? Of course, I may be mistaken; but—'

Ethel made pause, and looked Mrs Shepherd straight in the face. Smiling sadly, Mrs Shepherd said—

'Likenesses are so deceptive.'

'Perhaps, but my memory is pretty good for faces…. It was two or three months ago, we were going up to London, and I saw my brother get into the train with a lady who looked like you. She really was very like you.'

Mrs Shepherd smiled and shook her head.

'I do not know the lady my brother was with, but I've often thought I should like to meet her.'

'Perhaps your brother will introduce you.'

94

'No, I don't think he will. She has come to live at Branbury, and now people talk more then ever. They say that he is secretly married.'

'And you believe it?'

'I don't see why it shouldn't be true. My brother is a good fellow in many ways, but, like all other men, he is selfish. He is just the man who would keep his wife hidden away in a lonely little lodging rather than admit that he had made a mésalliance. What I don't understand is why she consents to be kept out of the way. Just fancy giving up this beautiful place, these woods and fields, these gardens, that house for, for—'

'I suppose this woman gives up these things because she loves your brother. Do you not understand self-sacrifice?'

'Oh yes, if I loved a man…. But I think a woman is silly to allow a man to cheat and fool her to the top of his bent.'

'What does it matter if she is happy?'

Ethel tossed her head. Then at the end of a long silence she said: 'Would you care to see the house?'

'No, thank you, Miss; I must be getting on. Goodbye.'

'You cannot get back that way, you must return through the pleasure-grounds. I'll walk with you. A headache kept me at home this afternoon. The others have gone to a tennis-party…. It is a pity I was mistaken. I should like to meet the person my brother goes every day to Branbury to see. I should like to talk with her. My brother has, I'm afraid, persuaded her that we would not receive her. But this is not true; we should only be too glad to receive her. I

95

have heard Father and Mother say so—not to Charles, they dare not speak to him on the subject, but they have to me.'

'Your brother must have some good reason for keeping his marriage secret. This woman may have a past.'

'Yes, they say that—but I should not care if I liked her, if I knew her to be a good woman now.'

To better keep the Major's secret, Mrs Shepherd had given up all friends, all acquaintance. She had not known a woman-friend for years, and the affinities of sex drew her to accept the sympathy with which she was tempted. The reaction of ten years of self-denial surged up within her, and she felt that she must speak, that her secret was being dragged from her. Ethel's eyes were fixed upon her—in another moment she would have spoken, but at that moment Nellie appeared climbing up the steep bank. 'Is that your little girl? Oh, what a pretty child!' Then raising her eyes from the child and looking the mother straight in the face, Ethel said—

'She is like, she is strangely like, Charles.'

Tears glistened in Mrs Shepherd's eyes, and then, no longer doubting that Mrs Shepherd would break down and in a flow of tears tell the whole story of her life, Ethel allowed a note of triumph to creep into her voice, and before she could stop herself she said, 'And that little girl is the heiress of Appleton Park.'

Mrs Shepherd's face changed expression.

'You are mistaken, Miss Shepherd,' she said; 'but if I ever meet your brother I will tell him that you think my little girl like him.'

Mrs Shepherd pursued her way slowly across the park, her long

96

weary figure showing upon the sunset, her black dress trailing on the crisp grass. Often she was obliged to pause; the emotion and exercise of the day had brought back pain, and her whole body thrilled with it. Since the birth of her child she had lived in pain. But as she leaned against the white gate, and looked back on the beautiful park never to be seen by her again, knowledge of her sacrifice quickened within her—the house and the park, and the manner and speech of the young girl, combined to help her to a full appreciation of all she had surrendered. She regretted nothing. However mean and obscure her life had been, it had contained at least one noble moment. Nellie pursued the dragonflies; Mrs Shepherd followed slowly, feeling like a victor in a great battle. She had not broken her trust; she had kept her promise intact; she would return to London tomorrow or next day, or at the end of the week, whenever the Major wished.

He was waiting for them at the corner of the lane, and Nellie was already telling him all she thought of the house, the woods, the flowers, and the lady who had sat down by Mother on the bench above the river. The Major looked at his wife in doubt and fear; her smile, however, reassured him. Soon after, Nellie fell asleep, and while she dreamed of butterflies and flowers Mrs Shepherd told him what had passed between her and his sister in the beechwood above the river.

'You see, what I told you was right. Your appearance has been described to them; they suspect something, and will never cease worrying until they have found out everything. I'm not a bit surprised. Ethel always was the more cunning and the more spiteful of the two.'

Mrs Shepherd did not tell him how nearly she had been betrayed into confession. She felt that he would not understand her explanation of the mood in which his sister had caught her. Men understand women so little. To tell him would be merely to destroy his confidence in her. As they drove through the twilight, with Nellie fast asleep between, he spoke of her departure, which he had arranged for the end of the week, and then, putting his arm round her waist, he said: 'You have always been a good little woman to me.'

# WALTER BESANT

# THE SOLID GOLD REEF COMPANY, LIMITED

(In Deacon's Orders and Other Stories, New York: Harper and Bros, 1895)

## Act I

'You dear old boy,' said the girl, 'I am sure I wish it could be, with all my heart, if I have any heart.'

'I don't believe you have,' replied the boy gloomily.

'Well, but, Reg, consider; you've got no money.'

'I've got five thousand pounds. If a man can't make his way upon that he must be a poor stick.'

'You would go abroad with it and dig, and take your wife with you—to wash and cook.'

'We would do something with the money here. You should stay in London, Rosie.'

'Yes. In a suburban villa, at Shepherd's Bush, perhaps. No, Reg, when I marry, if ever I do—I am in no hurry—I will step out of this room into one exactly like it.' The room was a splendid drawing-room in Palace Gardens, splendidly furnished. 'I shall have my footmen and my carriage, and I shall—'

'Rosie, give me the right to earn all these things for you!' the young man cried impetuously.

'You can only earn them for me by the time you have one foot in the grave. Hadn't I better in the meantime marry some old gentleman with his one foot in the grave, so as to be ready for you against the time you come home? In two or three years the other foot, I dare say, would slide into the grave as well.'

'You laugh at my trouble. You feel nothing.'

'If the pater would part, but he won't; he says he wants all his money for himself, and that I've got to marry well. Besides, Reg'— here her face clouded and she lowered her voice—'there are times when he looks anxious. We didn't always live in Palace Gardens. Suppose we should lose it all as quickly as we got it. Oh!' she shivered and trembled. 'No, I will never, never marry a poor man. Get rich, my dear boy, and you may aspire even to the valuable possession of this heartless hand.'

She held it out. He took it, pressed it, stooped and kissed her. Then he dropped her hand and walked quickly out of the room.

'Poor Reggie!' she murmured. 'I wish—I wish—but what is the use of wishing?'

# Act II

Two men—one young, the other about fifty—sat in the veranda of a small bungalow. It was after breakfast. They lay back in long bamboo chairs, each with a cigar. It looked as if they were resting. In reality they were talking business, and that very seriously.

'Yes, sir,' said the elder man, with something of an American accent, 'I have somehow taken a fancy to this place. The situation is healthy.'

'Well, I don't know; I've had more than one touch of fever here.'

'The climate is lovely—'

'Except in the rains.'

'The soil is fertile—'

'I've dropped five thousand in it, and they haven't come up again yet.'

'They will. I have been round the estate, and I see money in it. Well, sir, here's my offer: five thousand down, hard cash, as soon as the papers are signed.'

Reginald sat up. He was on the point of accepting the proposal, when a pony rode up to the house, and the rider, a native groom, jumped off and gave him a note. He opened it and read. It was from his nearest neighbour, two or three miles away:

Don't sell that man your estate. Gold has been found. The

101

whole country is full of gold. Hold on. He's an assayer. If he offers to buy, be quite sure that he has found gold on your land.

F.G.

He put the note into his pocket, gave a verbal message to the boy, and turned to his guest, without betraying the least astonisment or emotion.

'I beg your pardon. The note was from Bellamy, my next neighbour. Well? You were saying—'

'Only that I have taken a fancy—perhaps a foolish fancy—to this place of yours, and I'll give you, if you like, all that you have spent upon it.'

'Well,' he replied reflectively, but with a little twinkle in his eye, 'that seems handsome. But the place isn't really worth the half that I spent upon it. Anybody would tell you that. Come, let us be honest, whatever we are. I'll tell you a better way. We will put the matter into the hands of Bellamy. He knows what a coffee plantation is worth. He shall name a price, and if we can agree upon that, we will make a deal of it.'

The other man changed colour. He wanted to settle the thing at once as between gentlemen. What need of third parties? But Reginald stood firm, and he presently rode away, quite sure that in a day or two this planter, too, would have heard the news.

A month later, the young coffee-planter stood on the deck of a steamer homeward bound. In his pocket-book was a plan of his auriferous estate; in a bag hanging round his neck was a small collection of yellow nuggets; in his boxes was a chosen assortment of quartz.

# Act III

'Well, sir,' said the financier, 'you've brought this thing to me. You want my advice. Well, my advice is, don't fool away the only good thing that will ever happen to you. Luck such as this doesn't come more than once in a lifetime.'

'I have been offered ten thousand pounds for my estate.'

'Oh! Have you! Ten thousand? That was very liberal—very liberal indeed. Ten thousand for a gold reef!'

'But I thought as an old friend of my father you would, perhaps—'

'Young man, don't fool it away. He's waiting for you, I suppose, round the corner, with a bottle of fizz, ready to close.'

'He is.'

'Well, go and drink his champagne. Always get whatever you can. And then tell him that you'll see him—'

'I certainly will, sir, if you advise it. And then?'

'And then—leave it to me. And, young man, I think I heard, a year or two ago, something about you and my girl Rosie.'

103

'There was something, sir. Not enough to trouble you about it.'

'She told me. Rosie tells me all her love affairs.'

'Is she—is she unmarried?'

'Oh, yes! and for the moment I believe she is free. She has had one or two engagements, but, somehow, they have come to nothing. There was the French count, but that was knocked on the head very early in consequence of things discovered. And there was the Boom in Guano, but he fortunately smashed, much to Rosie's joy, because she never liked him. The last was Lord Evergreen. He was a nice old chap when you could understand what he said, and Rosie would have liked the title very much, though his grandchildren opposed the thing. Well, sir, I suppose you couldn't understand the trouble we took to keep that old man alive for his own wedding. Science did all it could, but 'twas of no use—' The financier sighed. 'The ways of Providence are inscrutable. He died, sir, the day before.'

'That was very sad.'

'A dashing of the cup from the lip, sir. My daughter would have been a countess. Well, young gentleman, about this estate of yours. I think I see a way—I think, I am not yet sure—that I do see a way. Go now. See this liberal gentleman, and drink his champagne. And come here in a week. Then, if I still see my way, you shall understand what it means to hold the position in the City which is mine.'

'And—and—may I call upon Rosie!'

'Not till this day week—not till I have made my way plain.'

# Act IV

'And so it means this. Oh, Rosie, you look lovelier than ever, and I'm as happy as a king. It means this. Your father is the greatest genius in the world. He buys my property for sixty thousand pounds—sixty thousand. That's over two thousand a year for me, and he makes a company out of it with a hundred and fifty thousand capital. He says that, taking ten thousand out of it for expenses, there will be a profit of eighty thousand. And all that he gives to you—eighty thousand, that's three thousand a year for you; and sixty thousand, that's two more, my dearest Rosie. You remember what you said, that when you married you should step out of one room like this into another just as good?'

'Oh, Reggie,' she sank upon his bosom—'you know I never could love anybody but you. It's true I was engaged to old Lord Evergreen, but that was only because he had one foot—you know— and when the other foot went in too, just a day too soon, I actually laughed. So the pater is going to make a company of it, is he? Well, I hope he won't put any of his own money into it, I'm sure, because of late all the companies have turned out so badly.'

'But, my child, the place is full of gold.'

'Then why did he turn it into a company, my dear boy? And why didn't he make you stick to it? But you know nothing of the City. Now, let us sit down and talk about what we shall do—don't, you ridiculous boy!'

# Act V

Another house just like the first. The bride stepped out of one palace into another. With their five or six thousand a year, the young couple could just manage to make both ends meet. The husband was devoted; the wife had everything that she could wish. Who could be happier than this pair in a nest so luxurious, their life so padded, their days so full of sunshine?

It was a year after marriage. The wife, contrary to her usual custom, was the first at breakfast. A few letters were waiting for her— chiefly invitations. She opened and read them. Among them lay one addressed to her husband. Not looking at the address, she opened and read that as well:

Dear Reginald:

I venture to address you as an old friend of your own and school-fellow of your mother's. I am a widow with four children. My husband was the vicar of your old parish— you remember him and me. I was left with a little income of about two hundred a year. Twelve months ago I was persuaded in order to double my income—a thing which seemed certain from the prospectus—to invest everything in a new and rich gold mine. Everything. And the mine has never paid anything. The company—it is called the Solid Gold Reef Company, is in liquidation because, though there is really the gold there, it costs too much to get it. I have no relatives anywhere to help me. Unless I can get assistance my children and I must go at once—tomorrow—into the workhouse. Yes, we are paupers. I am ruined by the cruel lies of that prospectus, and the wickedness which deluded me, and I know not how many others, out of my money. I have been foolish, and am punished; but those people, who will punish them? Help me, if you can, my dear Reginald. Oh! for GOD'S sake, help my children and me. Help your mother's friend, your own old friend.

'This,' said Rosie meditatively, 'is exactly the kind of thing to make Reggie uncomfortable. Why, it might make him unhappy all day. Better burn it.' She dropped the letter into the fire. 'He's an impulsive, emotional nature, and he doesn't understand the City. If people are so foolish—What a lot of fibs the poor old pater does tell, to be sure! He's a regular novelist—Oh! here you are, you lazy boy!'

'Kiss me, Rosie.' He looked as handsome as Apollo, and as cheerful. 'I wish all the world were as happy as you and me. Heigho! some poor devils, I'm afraid—'

'Tea or coffee, Reg?'

# HENRY JAMES

# THE TREE OF KNOWLEDGE

(The Soft Side, London: Methuen and Co, 1900)

# I

It was one of the secret opinions, such as we all have, of Peter
Brench that his main success in life would have consisted in his
never having committed himself about the work, as it was called, of
his friend Morgan Mallow. This was a subject on which it was, to
the best of his belief, impossible with veracity to quote him, and it
was nowhere on record that he had, in the connexion, on any
occasion and in any embarrassment, either lied or spoken the truth.
Such a triumph had its honour even for a man of other triumphs—a
man who had reached fifty, who had escaped marriage, who had
lived within his means, who had been in love with Mrs Mallow for
years without breathing it, and who, last but not least, had judged
himself once for all. He had so judged himself in fact that he felt an
extreme and general humility to be his proper portion; yet there
was nothing that made him think so well of his parts as the course
he had steered so often through the shallows just mentioned. It
became thus a real wonder that the friends in whom he had most
confidence were just those with whom he had most reserves. He

couldn't tell Mrs Mallow—or at least he supposed, excellent man, he couldn't—that she was the one beautiful reason he had never married; any more than he could tell her husband that the sight of the multiplied marbles in that gentleman's studio was an affliction of which even time had never blunted the edge. His victory, however, as I have intimated, in regard to these productions, was not simply in his not having let it out that he deplored them; it was, remarkably, in his not having kept it in by anything else.

The whole situation, among these good people, was verily a marvel, and there was probably not such another for a long way from the spot that engages us—the point at which the soft declivity of Hampstead began at that time to confess in broken accents to Saint John's Wood. He despised Mallow's statues and adored Mallow's wife, and yet was distinctly fond of Mallow, to whom, in turn, he was equally dear. Mrs Mallow rejoiced in the statues—though she preferred, when pressed, the busts; and if she was visibly attached to Peter Brench it was because of his affection for Morgan. Each loved the other moreover for the love borne in each case to Lancelot, whom the Mallows respectively cherished as their only child and whom the friend of their fireside identified as the third— but decidedly the handsomest—of his godsons. Already in the old years it had come to that—that no one, for such a relation, could possibly have occurred to any of them, even to the baby itself, but Peter. There was luckily a certain independence, of the pecuniary sort, all round: the Master could never otherwise have spent his solemn Wanderjahre in Florence and Rome, and continued by the Thames as well as by the Arno and the Tiber to add unpurchased group to group and model, for what was too apt to prove in the event mere love, fancy-heads of celebrities either too busy or too buried—too much of the age or too little of it—to sit. Neither could

Peter, lounging in almost daily, have found time to keep the whole complicated tradition so alive by his presence. He was massive but mild, the depositary of these mysteries—large and loose and ruddy and curly, with deep tones, deep eyes, deep pockets, to say nothing of the habit of long pipes, soft hats and brownish greyish weather-faded clothes, apparently always the same.

He had 'written', it was known, but had never spoken, never spoken in particular of that; and he had the air (since, as was believed, he continued to write) of keeping it up in order to have something more—as if he hadn't at the worst enough—to be silent about. Whatever his air, at any rate, Peter's occasional unmentioned prose and verse were quite truly the result of an impulse to maintain the purity of his taste by establishing still more firmly the right relation of fame to feebleness. The little green door of his domain was in a garden-wall on which the discoloured stucco made patches, and in the small detached villa behind it everything was old, the furniture, the servants, the books, the prints, the immemorial habits and the new improvements. The Mallows, at Carrara Lodge, were within ten minutes, and the studio there was on their little land, to which they had added, in their happy faith, for building it. This was the good fortune, if it was not the ill, of her having brought him in marriage a portion that put them in a manner at their ease and enabled them thus, on their side, to keep it up. And they did keep it up—they always had—the infatuated sculptor and his wife, for whom nature had refined on the impossible by relieving them of the sense of the difficult. Morgan had at all events everything of the sculptor but the spirit of Phidias—the brown velvet, the becoming beretto, the 'plastic' presence, the fine fingers, the beautiful accent in Italian and the old Italian factotum. He seemed to make up for everything when he

110

addressed Egidio with the 'tu' and waved him to turn one of the rotary pedestals of which the place was full. They were tremendous Italians at Carrara Lodge, and the secret of the part played by this fact in Peter's life was in a large degree that it gave him, sturdy Briton as he was, just the amount of 'going abroad' he could bear. The Mallows were all his Italy, but it was in a measure for Italy he liked them. His one worry was that Lance—to which they had shortened his godson—was, in spite of a public school, perhaps a shade too Italian. Morgan meanwhile looked like somebody's flattering idea of somebody's own person as expressed in the great room provided at the Uffizi Museum for the general illustration of that idea by eminent hands. The Master's sole regret that he hadn't been born rather to the brush than to the chisel sprang from his wish that he might have contributed to that collection.

It appeared with time at any rate to be to the brush that Lance had been born; for Mrs Mallow, one day when the boy was turning twenty, broke it to their friend, who shared, to the last delicate morsel, their problems and pains, that it seemed as if nothing would really do but that he should embrace the career. It had been impossible longer to remain blind to the fact that he was gaining no glory at Cambridge, where Brench's own college had for a year tempered its tone to him as for Brench's own sake. Therefore why renew the vain form of preparing him for the impossible? The impossible—it had become clear—was that he should be anything but an artist.

'Oh dear, dear!' said poor Peter.

'Don't you believe in it?' asked Mrs Mallow, who still, at more than forty, had her violet velvet eyes, her creamy satin skin and her silken chestnut hair.

'Believe in what?'

'Why in Lance's passion.'

'I don't know what you mean by "believing in it". I've never been unaware, certainly, of his disposition, from his earliest time, to daub and draw; but I confess I've hoped it would burn out.'

'But why should it,' she sweetly smiled, 'with his wonderful heredity? Passion is passion—though of course indeed you, dear Peter, know nothing of that. Has the Master's ever burned out?'

Peter looked off a little and, in his familiar formless way, kept up for a moment, a sound between a smothered whistle and a subdued hum. 'Do you think he's going to be another Master?'

She seemed scarce prepared to go that length, yet she had on the whole a marvellous trust. 'I know what you mean by that. Will it be a career to incur the jealousies and provoke the machinations that have been at times almost too much for his father? Well—say it may be, since nothing but clap-trap, in these dreadful days, can, it would seem, make its way, and since, with the curse of refinement and distinction, one may easily find one's self begging one's bread. Put it at the worst—say he has the misfortune to wing his flight further than the vulgar taste of his stupid countrymen can follow. Think, all the same, of the happiness—the same the Master has had. He'll know.'

Peter looked rueful. 'Ah but what will he know?'

'Quiet joy!' cried Mrs Mallow, quite impatient and turning away.

# II

He had of course before long to meet the boy himself on it and to hear that practically everything was settled. Lance was not to go up again, but to go instead to Paris where, since the die was cast, he would find the best advantages. Peter had always felt he must be taken as he was, but had never perhaps found him so much of that pattern as on this occasion. 'You chuck Cambridge then altogether? Doesn't that seem rather a pity?'

Lance would have been like his father, to his friend's sense, had he had less humour, and like his mother had he had more beauty. Yet it was a good middle way for Peter that, in the modern manner, he was, to the eye, rather the young stock-broker than the young artist. The youth reasoned that it was a question of time—there was such a mill to go through, such an awful lot to learn. He had talked with fellows and had judged. 'One has got, today,' he said, 'don't you see? to know.'

His interlocutor, at this, gave a groan. 'Oh hang it, don't know!'

Lance wondered. '"Don't"? Then what's the use—?'

'The use of what?'

'Why of anything. Don't you think I've talent?'

Peter smoked away for a little in silence; then went on: 'It isn't knowledge, it's ignorance that—as we've been beautifully told—is bliss.'

'Don't you think I've talent?' Lance repeated.

113

Peter, with his trick of queer kind demonstrations, passed his arm round his godson and held him a moment. 'How do I know?'

'Oh,' said the boy, 'if it's your own ignorance you're defending—!'

Again, for a pause, on the sofa, his godfather smoked. 'It isn't. I've the misfortune to be omniscient.'

'Oh well,' Lance laughed again, 'if you know too much—!'

'That's what I do, and it's why I'm so wretched.'

Lance's gaiety grew. 'Wretched? Come, I say!'

'But I forgot,' his companion went on—'you're not to know about that. It would indeed for you too make the too much. Only I'll tell you what I'll do.' And Peter got up from the sofa. 'If you'll go up again I'll pay your way at Cambridge.'

Lance stared, a little rueful in spite of being still more amused. 'Oh Peter! You disapprove so of Paris?'

'Well, I'm afraid of it.'

'Ah I see!'

'No, you don't see—yet. But you will—that is you would. And you mustn't.'

The young man thought more gravely. 'But one's innocence, already—!'

'Is considerably damaged? Ah that won't matter,' Peter persisted—'we'll patch it up here.'

'Here? Then you want me to stay at home?'

Peter almost confessed to it. 'Well, we're so right—we four together—just as we are. We're so safe. Come, don't spoil it.'

The boy, who had turned to gravity, turned from this, on the real pressure of his friend's tone, to consternation. 'Then what's a fellow to be?'

'My particular care. Come, old man'—and Peter now fairly pleaded—'I'll look out for you.'

Lance, who had remained on the sofa with his legs out and his hands in his pockets, watched him with eyes that showed suspicion. Then he got up. 'You think there's something the matter with me—that I can't make a success.'

'Well, what do you call a success?'

Lance thought again. 'Why the best sort, I suppose, is to please one's self. Isn't that the sort that, in spite of cabals and things, is—in his own peculiar line—the Master's?'

There were so much too many things in this question to be answered at once that they practically checked the discussion, which became particularly difficult in the light of such renewed proof that, though the young man's innocence might, in the course of his studies, as he contended, somewhat have shrunken, the finer essence of it still remained. That was indeed exactly what Peter had assumed and what above all he desired; yet perversely enough it gave him a chill. The boy believed in the cabals and things, believed in the peculiar line, believed, to be brief, in the Master. What happened a month or two later wasn't that he went up again at the expense of his godfather, but that a fortnight after he had got settled in Paris this personage sent him fifty pounds.

115

He had meanwhile at home, this personage, made up his mind to the worst; and what that might be had never yet grown quite so vivid to him as when, on his presenting himself one Sunday night, as he never failed to do, for supper, the mistress of Carrara Lodge met him with an appeal as to—of all things in the world—the wealth of the Canadians. She was earnest, she was even excited. 'Are many of them really rich?'

He had to confess he knew nothing about them, but he often thought afterwards of that evening. The room in which they sat was adorned with sundry specimens of the Master's genius, which had the merit of being, as Mrs Mallow herself frequently suggested, of an unusually convenient size. They were indeed of dimensions not customary in the products of the chisel, and they had the singularity that, if the objects and features intended to be small looked too large, the objects and features intended to be large looked too small. The Master's idea, either in respect to this matter or to any other, had in almost any case, even after years, remained undiscoverable to Peter Brench. The creations that so failed to reveal it stood about on pedestals and brackets, on tables and shelves, a little staring white population, heroic, idyllic, allegoric, mythic, symbolic, in which 'scale' had so strayed and lost itself that the public square and the chimney-piece seemed to have changed places, the monumental being all diminutive and the diminutive all monumental; branches at any rate, markedly, of a family in which stature was rather oddly irrespective of function, age and sex. They formed, like the Mallows themselves, poor Brench's own family— having at least to such a degree the note of familiarity. The occasion was one of those he had long ago learnt to know and to name— short flickers of the faint flame, soft gusts of a kinder air. Twice a year regularly the Master believed in his fortune, in addition to believing all the year round in his genius. This time it was to be made by a bereaved couple from Toronto, who had given him the handsomest order for a tomb to three lost children, each of whom they desired to see, in the composition, emblematically and characteristically represented.

Such was naturally the moral of Mrs Mallow's question: if their wealth was to be assumed, it was clear, from the nature of their admiration, as well as from mysterious hints thrown out (they were a little odd!) as to other possibilities of the same mortuary sort, what their further patronage might be; and not less evident that should the Master become at all known in those climes nothing would be more inevitable than a run of Canadian custom. Peter had been present before at runs of custom, colonial and domestic— present at each of those of which the aggregation had left so few gaps in the marble company round him; but it was his habit never at these junctures to prick the bubble in advance. The fond illusion, while it lasted, eased the wound of elections never won, the long ache of medals and diplomas carried off, on every chance, by everyone but the Master; it moreover lighted the lamp that would glimmer through the next eclipse. They lived, however, after all—as it was always beautiful to see—at a height scarce susceptible of ups and downs. They strained a point at times charmingly, strained it to admit that the public was here and there not too bad to buy; but they would have been nowhere without their attitude that the Master was always too good to sell. They were at all events deliciously formed, Peter often said to himself, for their fate; the Master had a vanity, his wife had a loyalty, of which success, depriving these things of innocence, would have diminished the merit and the grace. Anyone could be charming under a charm, and as he looked about him at a world of prosperity more void of

117

proportion even than the Master's museum he wondered if he knew another pair that so completely escaped vulgarity.

'What a pity Lance isn't with us to rejoice!' Mrs Mallow on this occasion sighed at supper.

'We'll drink to the health of the absent,' her husband replied, filling his friend's glass and his own and giving a drop to their companion; 'but we must hope he's preparing himself for a happiness much less like this of ours this evening—excusable as I grant it to be!—than like the comfort we have always (whatever has happened or has not happened) been able to trust ourselves to enjoy. The comfort,' the Master explained, leaning back in the pleasant lamplight and firelight, holding up his glass and looking round at his marble family, quartered more or less, a monstrous brood, in every room—'the comfort of art in itself!'

Peter looked a little shyly at his wine. 'Well—I don't care what you may call it when a fellow doesn't—but Lance must learn to sell, you know. I drink to his acquisition of the secret of a base popularity!'

'Oh yes, he must sell,' the boy's mother, who was still more, however, this seemed to give out, the Master's wife, rather artlessly allowed.

'Ah,' the sculptor after a moment confidently pronounced, 'Lance will. Don't be afraid. He'll have learnt.'

'Which is exactly what Peter,' Mrs Mallow gaily returned—'why in the world were you so perverse, Peter?—wouldn't, when he told him, hear of.'

Peter, when this lady looked at him with accusatory affection—a grace on her part not infrequent—could never find a word; but the

118

Master, who was always all amenity and tact, helped him out now as he had often helped him before. 'That's his old idea, you know—on which we've so often differed: his theory that the artist should be all impulse and instinct. I go in of course for a certain amount of school. Not too much—but a due proportion. There's where his protest came in,' he continued to explain to his wife, 'as against what might, don't you see? be in question for Lance.'

'Ah well'—and Mrs Mallow turned the violet eyes across the table at the subject of this discourse—'he's sure to have meant of course nothing but good. Only that wouldn't have prevented him, if Lance had taken his advice, from being in effect horribly cruel.'

They had a sociable way of talking of him to his face as if he had been in the clay or—at most—in the plaster, and the Master was unfailingly generous. He might have been waving Egidio to make him revolve. 'Ah but poor Peter wasn't so wrong as to what it may after all come to that he will learn.'

'Oh but nothing artistically bad,' she urged—still, for poor Peter, arch and dewy.

'Why just the little French tricks,' said the Master: on which their friend had to pretend to admit, when pressed by Mrs Mallow, that these æsthetic vices had been the objects of his dread.

## III

'I know now,' Lance said to him the next year, 'why you were so

119

much against it.' He had come back supposedly for a mere interval and was looking about him at Carrara Lodge, where indeed he had already on two or three occasions since his expatriation briefly reappeared. This had the air of a longer holiday. 'Something rather awful has happened to me. It isn't so very good to know.'

'I'm bound to say high spirits don't show in your face,' Peter was rather ruefully forced to confess. 'Still, are you very sure you do know?'

'Well, I at least know about as much as I can bear.' These remarks were exchanged in Peter's den, and the young man, smoking cigarettes, stood before the fire with his back against the mantel. Something of his bloom seemed really to have left him.

Poor Peter wondered. 'You're clear then as to what in particular I wanted you not to go for?'

'In particular?' Lance thought. 'It seems to me that in particular there can have been only one thing.'

They stood for a little sounding each other. 'Are you quite sure?'

'Quite sure I'm a beastly duffer? Quite—by this time.'

'Oh!'—and Peter turned away as if almost with relief.

'It's that that isn't pleasant to find out.'

'Oh I don't care for "that",' said Peter, presently coming round again. 'I mean I personally don't.'

'Yet I hope you can understand a little that I myself should!'

'Well, what do you mean by it?' Peter sceptically asked.

And on this Lance had to explain—how the upshot of his studies in Paris had inexorably proved a mere deep doubt of his means. These studies had so waked him up that a new light was in his eyes; but what the new light did was really to show him too much. 'Do you know what's the matter with me? I'm too horribly intelligent. Paris was really the last place for me. I've learnt what I can't do.'

Poor Peter stared—it was a staggerer; but even after they had had, on the subject, a longish talk in which the boy brought out to the full the hard truth of his lesson, his friend betrayed less pleasure than usually breaks into a face to the happy tune of 'I told you so!' Poor Peter himself made now indeed so little a point of having told him so that Lance broke ground in a different place a day or two after. 'What was it then that—before I went—you were afraid I should find out?' This, however, Peter refused to tell him—on the ground that if he hadn't yet guessed perhaps he never would, and that in any case nothing at all for either of them was to be gained by giving the thing a name. Lance eyed him on this an instant with the bold curiosity of youth—with the air indeed of having in his mind two or three names, of which one or other would be right. Peter nevertheless, turning his back again, offered no encouragement, and when they parted afresh it was with some show of impatience on the side of the boy. Accordingly on their next encounter Peter saw at a glance that he had now, in the interval, divined and that, to sound his note, he was only waiting till they should find themselves alone. This he had soon arranged and he then broke straight out. 'Do you know your conundrum has been keeping me awake? But in the watches of the night the answer came over me— so that, upon my honour, I quite laughed out. Had you been supposing I had to go to Paris to learn that? Even now, to see him still so sublimely on his guard, Peter's young friend had to laugh

121

afresh. 'You won't give a sign till you're sure? Beautiful old Peter!' But Lance at last produced it. 'Why, hang it, the truth about the Master.'

It made between them for some minutes a lively passage, full of wonder for each at the wonder of the other. 'Then how long have you understood—'

'The true value of his work? I understood it,' Lance recalled, 'as soon as I began to understand anything. But I didn't begin fully to do that, I admit, till I got là-bas.'

'Dear, dear!'—Peter gasped with retrospective dread.

'But for what have you taken me? I'm a hopeless muff—that I had to have rubbed in. But I'm not such a muff as the Master!' Lance declared.

'Then why did you never tell me—?'

'That I hadn't, after all'—the boy took him up—'remained such an idiot? Just because I never dreamed you knew. But I beg your pardon. I only wanted to spare you. And what I don't now understand is how the deuce then for so long you've managed to keep bottled.'

Peter produced his explanation, but only after some delay and with a gravity not void of embarrassment. 'It was for your mother.'

'Oh!' said Lance.

'And that's the great thing now—since the murder is out. I want a promise from you. I mean'—and Peter almost feverishly followed it up—'a vow from you, solemn and such as you owe me here on the spot, that you'll sacrifice anything rather than let her ever guess—'

'That I've guessed?'—Lance took it in. 'I see.' He evidently after a moment had taken in much. 'But what is it you've in mind that I may have a chance to sacrifice?'

'Oh one has always something.'

Lance looked at him hard. 'Do you mean that you've had—?' The look he received back, however, so put the question by that he found soon enough another. 'Are you really sure my mother doesn't know?'

Peter, after renewed reflexion, was really sure. 'If she does she's too wonderful.'

'But aren't we all too wonderful?'

'Yes,' Peter granted—'but in different ways. The thing's so desperately important because your father's little public consists only, as you know then,' Peter developed—'well, of how many?'

'First of all,' the Master's son risked, 'of himself. And last of all too. I don't quite see of whom else.'

Peter had an approach to impatience. 'Of your mother, I say— always.'

Lance cast it all up. 'You absolutely feel that?'

'Absolutely.'

'Well then with yourself that makes three.'

'Oh me!'—and Peter, with a wag of his kind old head, modestly excused himself. The number's at any rate small enough for any individual dropping out to be too dreadfully missed. Therefore, to put it in a nutshell, take care, my boy—that's all—that you're not!'

123

'I've got to keep on humbugging?' Lance wailed.

'It's just to warn you of the danger of your failing of that that I've seized this opportunity.'

'And what do you regard in particular,' the young man asked, 'as the danger?'

'Why this certainty: that the moment your mother, who feels so strongly, should suspect your secret—well,' said Peter desperately, 'the fat would be on the fire.'

Lance for a moment seemed to stare at the blaze. 'She'd throw me over?'

'She'd throw him over.'

'And come round to us?'

Peter, before he answered, turned away. 'Come round to you.' But he had said enough to indicate—and, as he evidently trusted, to avert—the horrid contingency.

# IV

Within six months again, none the less, his fear was on more occasions than one all before him. Lance had returned to Paris for another trial; then had reappeared at home and had had, with his father, for the first time in his life, one of the scenes that strike sparks. He described it with much expression to Peter, touching

124

whom (since they had never done so before) it was the sign of a new reserve on the part of the pair at Carrara Lodge that they at present failed, on a matter of intimate interest, to open themselves—if not in joy then in sorrow—to their good friend. This produced perhaps practically between the parties a shade of alienation and a slight intermission of commerce—marked mainly indeed by the fact that to talk at his ease with his old playmate Lance had in general to come to see him. The closest if not quite the gayest relation they had yet known together was thus ushered in. The difficulty for poor Lance was a tension at home—begotten by the fact that his father wished him to be at least the sort of success he himself had been. He hadn't 'chucked' Paris—though nothing appeared more vivid to him than that Paris had chucked him: he would go back again because of the fascination in trying, in seeing, in sounding the depths—in learning one's lesson, briefly, even if the lesson were simply that of one's impotence in the presence of one's larger vision. But what did the Master, all aloft in his senseless fluency, know of impotence, and what vision—to be called such—had he in all his blind life ever had? Lance, heated and indignant, frankly appealed to his godparent on this score.

His father, it appeared, had come down on him for having, after so long, nothing to show, and hoped that on his next return this deficiency would be repaired. The thing, the Master complacently set forth was—for any artist, however inferior to himself—at least to 'do' something. 'What can you do? That's all I ask!' He had certainly done enough, and there was no mistake about what he had to show. Lance had tears in his eyes when it came thus to letting his old friend know how great the strain might be on the 'sacrifice' asked of him. It wasn't so easy to continue humbugging— as from son to parent—after feeling one's self despised for not

125

grovelling in mediocrity. Yet a noble duplicity was what, as they intimately faced the situation, Peter went on requiring; and it was still for a time what his young friend, bitter and sore, managed loyally to comfort him with. Fifty pounds more than once again, it was true, rewarded both in London and in Paris the young friend's loyalty; none the less sensibly, doubtless, at the moment, that the money was a direct advance on a decent sum for which Peter had long since privately prearranged an ultimate function. Whether by these arts or others, at all events, Lance's just resentment was kept for a season—but only for a season—at bay. The day arrived when he warned his companion that he could hold out—or hold in—no longer. Carrara Lodge had had to listen to another lecture delivered from a great height—an infliction really heavier at last than, without striking back or in some way letting the Master have the truth, flesh and blood could bear.

'And what I don't see is,' Lance observed with a certain irritated eye for what was after all, if it came to that, owing to himself too; 'what I don't see is, upon my honour, how you, as things are going, can keep the game up.'

'Oh the game for me is only to hold my tongue,' said placid Peter. 'And I have my reason.'

'Still my mother?'

Peter showed a queer face as he had often shown it before—that is by turning it straight away. 'What will you have? I haven't ceased to like her.'

'She's beautiful—she's a dear of course,' Lance allowed; 'but what is she to you, after all, and what is it to you that, as to anything whatever, she should or she shouldn't?'

126

Peter, who had turned red, hung fire a little. 'Well—it's all simply what I make of it.'

There was now, however, in his young friend a strange, an adopted insistence. 'What are you after all to her?'

'Oh nothing. But that's another matter.'

'She cares only for my father,' said Lance the Parisian.

'Naturally—and that's just why.'

'Why you've wished to spare her?'

'Because she cares so tremendously much.'

Lance took a turn about the room, but with his eyes still on his host. 'How awfully—always—you must have liked her!'

'Awfully. Always,' said Peter Brench.

The young man continued for a moment to muse—then stopped again in front of him. 'Do you know how much she cares?' Their eyes met on it, but Peter, as if his own found something new in Lance's, appeared to hesitate, for the first time in an age, to say he did know. 'I've only just found out,' said Lance. 'She came to my room last night, after being present, in silence and only with her eyes on me, at what I had had to take from him: she came—and she was with me an extraordinary hour.'

He had paused again and they had again for a while sounded each other. Then something—and it made him suddenly turn pale—came to Peter. 'She does know?'

'She does know. She let it all out to me—so as to demand of me no more than "that", as she said, of which she herself had been capable. She has always, always known,' said Lance without pity.

Peter was silent a long time; during which his companion might have heard him gently breathe, and on touching him might have felt within him the vibration of a long low sound suppressed. By the time he spoke at last he had taken everything in. 'Then I do see how tremendously much.'

'Isn't it wonderful?' Lance asked.

'Wonderful,' Peter mused.

'So that if your original effort to keep me from Paris was to keep me from knowledge—!' Lance exclaimed as if with a sufficient indication of this futility.

It might have been at the futility Peter appeared for a little to gaze. 'I think it must have been—without my quite at the time knowing it—to keep me!' he replied at last as he turned away.

www.ingramcontent.com/pod-product-compliance
Lightning Source LLC
Chambersburg PA
CBHW011515170626
46810CB00009B/3374